Bizarro 101:
A Basic Primer
(37 Flash Fiction Stories)

BY WOL-VRIEY

Other Books By Wol-vriey:

The Bizarro Story of I

Meat Suitcase

Chainsaw Cop Corpse

Vegan Zombie Apocalypse

Boston Posh

Vegan Vampire Vaginas

Vagina Mundi

Melanie Nemesis Catchpole

**Novellas and Short Stories By
Wol-vriey:**

Big Trouble in Little Ass
A novella featured in
Westward Hoes

Forever Ago Sunshine
A short story featured in
The Big Book of Bizarro

Bizarro 101:
A Basic Primer
(37 Flash Fiction Stories)

BY WOL-VRIEY

Burning Bulb
PUBLISHING

Bizarro 101: A Basic Primer
By **Wol-vriey**

Burning Bulb Publishing
P.O. Box 4721
Bridgeport, WV 26330-4721
United States of America
www.BurningBulbPublishing.com

Cover designed by Gary Lee Vincent with the following licensed elements:
- Image # 154165721 © Valentina Photos | Shutterstock.com

Author Photo: Lolade Akinsowon © 2014

First Edition.

Paperback Edition ISBN: 978-0692419007

Printed in the United States of America

The following stories have all been previously published (online or in print) elsewhere:

- *Angie Stone's Revival* in 'A Quick Bite of Flesh' (Hazardous Press)
- *Soft Silky Skin* in 'Hell Whore Vol. 3' (Horrified Press)
- *Love + Lust in Brazil* in Medulla Review Vol. 2, Issue #3 (http://www.themedullarcview.com)
- *Jackie Chan Angel* in The Moustache Factor (http://mustachefactor.blogspot.com)
- *Identia* in Three Minute Plastic (http://threeminuteplasticmag.blogspot.com)
- *Penisthumb* on Bizarro Central. (www.bizarrocentral.com)
- *Entertaining Spider, Venice, Ring Ring, The Original, Retro Race Relationship Rumbles, A Day At The Racists, Behind Every ~~Successful~~ Woman, The Original, The East Side of the House, Can't See For the Rain,* all previously appeared in the New Flesh webzine. (http://newfleshmagazine.blogspot.com)

Contents

Acknowledgements

Firstly, thanks to Gary Lee Vincent, Rich Bottles Jr., my lovely wife Victoria, William Pauley III, Kris Lugosi . . . lots of everyone elses who I can't immediately remember (don't worry, there'll be other books ☺).

Okay now, some credit for this: Teresa Pollack (who also helped proofread this anthology) came up with the basic idea for the title in a group letter which she posted to the Goodreads Bizarro Group.

For about a year previous to her letter, I'd had a similar idea for an anthology of my short fiction, with a similar title, but I kept putting it off, then putting it off some more; mainly because I couldn't decide on which stories of mine to compile—there's quite a lot of them kicking up dust everywhere.

But Teresa's Bizarro Group letter got me thinking about doing the collection again. But I still couldn't figure out which stories to include in it.

Then I woke up one morning with the idea of assembling all my flash fiction tales . . . and so this Bizarro 101 anthology was finally born.

Weird thing is: up till I began collating them, I honestly had no idea I'd written this many flash fiction shorts.

Enjoy the ride!

Wol-vriey (3/20/2015)

Introduction
by Teresa Pollack

Wol-vriey is widely known in the Bizarro community as 'the guy that writes really long books.' You either know him and love him, or you simply haven't heard of him. There doesn't appear to be an in-between—I've never came across anyone familiar with his work that *doesn't* enjoy his writing. He's also incredibly prolific, churning out large tomes roughly every year or so. And while he has had several shorts published, even they tend to be lengthier. So much, in fact, his *Westward Hoes* contribution, 'Big Trouble in Little Ass,' was released as a stand-alone novella. Obviously, being concise doesn't *appear* to be Wol-vriey's cup 'o tea.

So when I received an e-mail asking if I'd be interested in proofing this new book, I almost keeled over. Once my 'fan-girl syndrome' abated, and my wits returned, I re-read the e-mail. And I discovered that this book was actually not a book at all, but rather a collection of flash fiction. Flash fiction. From Wol-vriey. Hmmmmm….

At this point, I'm wondering if Wol-vriey has finally gone insane. After all, we're talking about **the** master of lengthy Bizarro novels, and now he's trying his hand at a flash fiction collection? *"How will this possibly turn out?"* I mused aloud. *"Can he actually pull this off?"* I continued to ponder, asking myself *"Will this be good, as in Wol-vriey style **good**?"* Well, the short answer is YES. Turns out, Wol-vriey is an all around genius! It's like the guy never misses! And he has outdone himself yet again.

This primer is the very essence of any and all styles and types of Bizarro writing. Wol-vriey collects, distills, and bottles up these 37 tiny stories for your sensory enjoyment. This is an absolute must-read for anyone new to the genre, because it demonstrates the scope of what Bizarro is, and what it can be.

Reading Wol-vriey can be a caustic, joyous, confusing, exhilarating, empowering, and terrifying roller coaster ride. While reading these pieces, I experienced the full gamut of emotions, leading me to feel like a schizoid two weeks off meds (I mean that in the best possible sense, of course). From the genius wordplay (honestly, how many authors can construct a 3 page story in which every single word starts with the same letter?), to the endless puns, to the childlike relish with which he plays with trademarks, clear on down to the various perspectives (including second person), he simply masters it all. And not only technically, either. We're talking about phenomenal character development. Aliens, car-men, walking talking 'toon-goons,' and even some recurring characters—all these and then some pop up throughout these stories. Then you've got the plotlines and subject matter. These stories range from religion, politics, gender relations, comedy, tragedy, and then back again, racing along together, and occasionally meshing together in the same story. Each piece packs one hell of a punch, so together they create a truly deadly force.

And though I mention politics, and race, and other 'serious' topics, I really don't think Wol-vriey gives a shit if his readers choose to focus on that element of his work or not. It's not vital to the enjoyment of the work. Sure 'A Day At the Racists' could be taken **very** seriously. But me? Well, mostly I just laughed. I see the hypocrisy; I enjoy the depth; I feel the irony, but Wol-vriey's writing has a way of making me feel better about this fucked up world we live in. He makes it tolerable. Or maybe I just forget about it for a while because his work pulls me in so completely. Whatever it is, it works. There are several other standouts, including 'The Original,' 'Teething troubles,' 'Ahmed Apple,' etc. (and these are a *small* portion of my favorites), but you really just need to read them for yourself to understand what I mean.

Overall, this collection is a mish-mash of twisted fables, over-hauled fairy-tales, inexplicable events in 'normal' worlds, 'normal' events in inexplicable worlds, mind-boggling vignettes, piebald parables, and every other type of story in between. Wol-vriey is already *the* master of long Bizarro; this piece proves he also deserves the 'flash fiction phenom' moniker. Reminiscent of Violet LeVoit,

Mykle Hansen, and all those other 'smart' Bizarros, Wol-vriey has created a collection that is funny and goofy, while still throwing in serious undertones and deep takeaways. Read the stories as in depth or topically as you prefer. But first and foremost, HAVE FUN!!!! Now buckle those seatbelts, kids! You're about to go on one hell of a ride!

The Original

"I'm sick of this crap," Georg said. "I'd kill myself if I weren't already dead."

"And in Hell," the walls whispered in completion. *"Never forget that—you're DEAD and IN HELL."*

Georg sighed; at random he picked a Block out of the 'Plot' box and read the words cut into its corpse-flesh: 'Then the president had a burst of inspiration: what if she . . .'

He shook his head, dropped it, picked out another: '"It can't be true," she gasped, "she's *pregnant!!?*"'

Georg nodded, this was better, more in fitting with the tale he was 'making' for David Heilberg.

He pulled the 'composition' box towards him, examining and tagging the bits he'd already got. So far Doctor Mary O'Blige had come home to find her father dead, had been chased down a dark alley by a werewolf, and had had her little brother kidnapped by the French terrorist underground. Now she'd just discovered her boyfriend Inspector Hardcop had gotten her best friend pregnant.

Feeling like he was being emotionally castrated, Georg resumed 'making' Dave Heilberg's next bestseller.

One Hundred Years Earlier

"Look," Georg told Beetle-Pie, the UGLY-AS-HELL demon he'd just summoned, "I want the gift of *originality*. I'm a writer, but no matter how hard I try, I can't think up anything that hasn't been done before. My last four books were all panned for being derivative; worse—they sold worse than expired milk. So I want—"

"Originality? There's no such thing, Georg."

"There is," Georg said defiantly. "I've often come up with—"

"Recycled versions of everyone else's stories." The demon laughed, picking his teeth with a bloodstained fingernail. "Let's simplify things, okay? *All* you want is originality?"

"Georg recognized the trap. "They've also got to sell BIG TIME."

Beetle-Pie pulled a briefcase out of his belly and rummaged in it a while. Finally, he extracted a paperback novel and handed it to Georg. "Your next book."

"I said I want to *create* it, dammit; are you *deaf!?*"

Beetle-Pie's smile faded." You *will* create it, Georg; you *will*. You'll NEVER once remember this conversation, this . . . contract . . . until it's pay-up time."

"Gimme that bullshi . . ." He snatched the book out of the demon's hand and irritatedly flipped through, quickly growing more and more enamored with its contents. He finally stopped, stared at the demon in total stupefaction. "It's *fantastic*," he stuttered, "exactly what I've always wanted to write . . . the characters . . . the plot . . . the setting . . . Pulitzer prize shit for real." He smiled apologetically at Beetle-Pie. "Look, dude, I'm sorry bout all that crap I spouted earlier. Let's do the deal okay . . . *Okay?*"

Beetle-Pie smiled thinly. He'd been through this routine with so many writers through the ages.

"And now as regards payment . . ."

"Oh, to Hell with that," Georg said hastily, already living on Literary Olympus, "For a lifetime of *this*, I'll sign anything . . . anything."

"Fair enough," Beetle-Pie snickered, with a flourish pulling a smoking contract out of his left nostril. "If you'd please append your signature here . . . and here . . . and, oh yes, here."

***

It HAD been good. Georg had NO regrets. He'd won award after award, travelled the world, made MONEY. And died PEACEFULLY in bed at the age of ninety-three.

And immediately he'd closed his eyes that final time he'd found himself . . . in HELL.

***

"So what now?" he asked Beetle-Pie with trepidation, all memory of his lifetime successes already falling away like discarded clothes. "Am I in for an eternity of torment?"

"Something *like* that, Georg," the demon replied with an enigmatic smile, remembering he disliked Georg. "Something *very* like that."

He led Georg to a large room and pointed to a pile of packing crates and plastic cartons. "You're just going to *make* up stories."

"Oh that's easy," Georg breathed in relief, "that's ea . . ." In shock he realized he couldn't think up a single plot; not an idea came into his mind.

"It *is* easy," Beetle-Pie said with relish. "The crates and cartons contain Writer's Blocks; they're all organized by plot, character, scene . . . in some cases even by writer, if they've a contract with us. Consider them a puzzle, you just put the pieces together, anyhow you like. Once you've made a complete book, we find an author it fits and . . ."

"*Make books for other authors?*" Georg's dead face creased into a frown. "No way in Hell am I making stories for another's glory. Let the uncreative hacks do their own legwork."

Beetle-Pie smiled nastily. "Don't be selfish George—how'd you think we got the bestsellers we gave *you*? Besides, if you *don't* do it, we'll chop *you* into Writer's Blocks for other writers to assemble."

He vanished in a puff of ochre smoke.

Defeated, Georg walked over to the 'Plot' box and pulled out a quivering cube. It seemed made of human flesh. He turned it over, read the script engraved into it:

'Hard-as-nails C.I.A. operative Blake Hammer . . .'

Georg nodded, he liked the name 'Hammer.' He picked out another Block: 'Then Jack and the rabbit . . .' He dropped it back, picked out another: 'The aliens landed and blew up New Moscow . . .' That too seemed good to Georg . . . but so far, no women in the story. He began rooting amongst the 'Female Love Interest' Writer's Blocks: 'Melanie raised her gun and spat . . .'

***

Sitting in darkness much MUCH later, Georg wept. "I wish, just wish, I could create something original. *Anything*—just not spend eternity as a hack . . ."

"*Georg*," the walls whispered softly back, "*there's no such thing as true originality.*"

Penisthumb

On his twenty-fifth birthday, Jack cut off his right ear and stuck it in a pickle jar.

"You are my god," he said. "I have created you and I will worship you."

Jack created god because he felt only divinity could truly understand him. His disgust with organized religion however meant he lacked a ready-made deity to turn to.

Activated by Jack's desire, his right ear, submerged in vinegar, became self-aware, became EAR.

"How will you worship me?" EAR asked Jack.

"I will complain to you; my gripes are the sacrifices you must love."

"It is not right that you, my supplicant, dictate to me," EAR said. "I would prefer McDonald's occasionally."

"Do not develop ambitions beyond your station in life," Jack retorted. "You are my god, created to listen to me." He thought awhile, then added. "And occasionally to perform miracles."

"You are selfish," EAR said.

"Religion's a bitch," Jack replied. "Deal with it."

Time visited and left.

"I'm lonely and no one understands me," Jack told EAR. "Do what other gods do for their worshippers. Make me a helper meet for me."

So EAR created Jill for Jack.

She was tall and willowy, and looked like Julia Roberts in 1988.

"Oh, pretty woman!" Jack shouted, running across the room at her, arms raised in euphoria that he was no longer alone.

"*What the hell did you do that for!?*" he screamed piteously moments later, blood running down his legs from his burst testicles, exploded because Jill had violently kicked them.

"Keep your hands to yourself, pig!" she said coldly as he crumpled to the floor, "Just like you, I like *girls*. Next time I'll cut your dick off!"

In indescribable agony, Jack stared at his god in disbelief. "What the . . . you made me a *gay* woman?"

"Your faith in me was insufficient for heterosexuality, my child," EAR replied him.

"What is *that*!? Jill gasped, about freaking out from noticing the speaking ear in the pickle jar. "Are you a friggin' serial killer?"

"That's *god*," Jack whimpered. "Kneel and worship it. Feed it your complaints. Then ask it for whatever you desire."

"I'm misunderstood and no one loves me," Jill told EAR. "Make me a partner."

EAR sighed, wearied by the obtuse insatiability of its supplicants. It switched the location of Jack's penis from his crotch to his right hand, replacing his thumb with it. It also moved his exploded testicles to his chest, inflating them into breasts.

"Now you're remade in my image," Jill told Jack. "You're a woman like me, and I love you." She giggled. "I will call you Penisthumb."

So Penisthumb and Jill lived in peace and harmony for a full year, with Penisthumb thumbscrewing Jill twice daily, like properly taking one's medication.

And whenever Penisthumb emailed, she stuck her mouse between her legs, so her displaced right thumb could work it for her.

***

A year after Penisthumb and Jill had fallen madly in love, Dog appeared in the sky over New and Improved York City. Dog was HUGE and black and evil, and had twin rocket launcher turrets in place of nostrils.

"I Dog rule over all," it barked. "Bow before me, earthlings."

"In a pig's eye, asshole," the New and Improved Yorkers replied.

Incensed by their lack of reverence, Dog began shooting everyone, firing exploding Canadians from its nostril cannons.

Penisthumb was killed when a fusillade of Dog's Keanu-Reeves-rockets blew up the train she was commuting home from work in.

"DO SOMETHING!!!" Jill, tears streaming down her face, screamed at EAR once the hospital informed her of Penisthumb's death. "Avenge your creator!"

"I will fight and defeat this menace," EAR replied her. "Not for Penisthumb, but for *myself*. When I win, *all* humanity will worship ME. No longer will I be America's best kept secret!"

It flew out of the house, becoming bigger than Madison Square Garden, and engaged Dog in conflict over New and Improved York.

EAR fired earwax ICBMs at Dog, but Dog was faster. It blew the wax missiles apart with its Canadian patriots.

Sizzling wax droplets rained on the world, frying everyone they hit.

Everyone, Jill included, realized Judgment Day had finally arrived.

Though EAR fought bravely, it lacked Dog's killer instinct.

Dog killed EAR—after first blocking it with gorgeous Celine Dion clones (who ruptured its eardrum with their razor-pitched voices), it ripped EAR to pieces and wolfed it down.

Finally it descended to Earth.

"I am Dog," it said. "You will worship me."

"We cannot worship a *dog*," the New and Improved Yorkers patiently explained. "You lack *sophistication*; the Roman Catholics will mock us."

"Then I will reverse the spelling of my name and become *God* instead," Dog said.

"If you do this, you will be remade in our image, and *we will* worship you," the New and Improved Yorkers replied.

"And your previous gods?"

"They are of no consequence," the New and Improved York multitudes replied unequivocally. "We will nullify them with talk shows."

So Dog reversed its name and became God, and its form altered till it was human, and dressed in a tan Giorgio Armani Suit.

But once human, its powers left it. It became an ordinary man.

And Jill, realizing God was now powerless, and seeing her chance to avenge Penisthumb's death, screamed. "FAKER! CRUCIFY HIM!!!"

And the multitudes crucified God, bearing him above their heads to the banks of the Hudson River and nailing him to a tree there.

And God withered down to an elephant ear, with beautiful black roses growing around its rim. And in time and in turn, its roses also withered, because no one remembered to water them.

***

"My partner Penisthumb was a good woman," Jill said afterwards. "We will bury her, but keep her penis-thumb. This we will stick in a pickle jar and worship as our new god."

And the multitudes agreed. And all those who didn't were persecuted and sacrificed to PENISTHUMB.

Love + Lust in Brazil

You sit at a table in Club Cabana, listening to the aromatic sounds of Ricardo Puente et Los Familias. Opposite you sits Carmelita Del Rio, a golden-skinned Latina beauty with eyes like smoldering brownie campfires.

"Love only me," Carmelita insists.

She dissolves her face into a wineglass and hands it to you. "Drink it," she says. "This is my beauty."

You stare at the swirling mix of eyes, nose, ears, and eyelashes in blood and mucus, and take a hesitant sip, then drink deeply. Carmelita's beauty is a heady liquor.

(Rather than descend to your belly however, Carmelita's looks go to your head, where they stage a coup d'état and take over your emotional landscape. You feel her eyes, her nose, her loveliness, razing your opposition to her charms into ash and desolate brainland.)

Their blitz is successful—though faceless, Carmelita Del Rio is now the most lovely woman in the world to you.

"I love you," you say. Truthfully.

Carmelita next blends both her breasts and her heart, and pours them out for you to drink also. "Drink these as well, my darling. These are my feelings for you."

Now much bolder, you drain the pink yoghurt mixture. It goes down the right way, smooth as honey.

(You tremble, however, as in your head, her lipstick and lashes rape and massacre the ghosts of your former lovers.)

She pours you another glass of her feelings.

In the background Ricardo Puente's lady singer hits a particularly high note during her solo. Your second glass of Carmelita's breasts and heart shatters, spilling her emotions all over you.

Carmelita smiles a lipless ghoul's smile at you. "Love only me," she repeats.

The shattering of the wineglass has however shattered the spell she's cast over you.

(In your head, your senses slowly come to themselves. Guerilla torrents of lust ride nightmares through love-ravaged cities in battles to oust the invading gorgeousnesses.)

At that moment you notice Flavia Carlos walking by, swaying to the band.

Flavia is more beautiful that Carmelita. She is now single again. You know this because you murdered her boyfriend Ronaldo to make her single again.

Carmelita Del Rio notices you noticing Flavia Carlos. Her eyeless eyes narrow, the edges of her lipless mouth swoop down into a frown.

Flavia Carlos notices you noticing her, but not Carmelita Del Rio noticing both of you noticing each other. She smiles back.

"Pig!" Carmelita screams. She pulls a gun from her purse and shoots you in the face. Your brains and her face explode out the back of your head, spraying all over the Argentinian couple dining behind you.

Carmelita stands up. "Excuse me a minute," she says politely to the Argentinians. "I need to collect my looks."

She retrieves her eyes, ears, nose, fake lashes, painfully plucked eyebrows, and cherry-lipsticked lips from amidst their dinner, their hair, their clothes, and your splattered brains.

She reassembles her face on her face and returns back to you. You're lying on the floor, dying, to Ricardo Puente's singer cooing 'The Girl from Ipanema.'

Carmelita gets a nail file from her purse. She slits your belly with it, yanks out your stomach, and pours out her liquefied breasts and heart from it. She sculpts the organs back into shape again, and replaces them on and in her body.

"I sentence you to death for not loving me only," she says, raising her gun to properly kill you.

Flavia Carlos breaks a bottle of Moet et Chandon over her head. Carmelita slumps to the ground unconscious. She is dragged off and thrown out into the rain by the club bouncers.

Flavia peers down concernedly at you. She lovingly retrieves the chunks of your brain splattered all over the Argentinian couple.

Most of your brains are found and stuffed back into your head. Olives and cherries and coconut chunks from the bar are used to fill up the remaining headspace, and lemon peel is used like plumber's hemp, to pack both entrance and exit wounds of the bullet.

Revived, you sit down opposite Flavia Carlos, glad that your wet dreams of her are finally coming true.

Flavia pulls out a long, long, cigarette holder from her purse. Next she pulls out a gold lighter.

You curse yourself for not offering to light her cigarette.

But she's not planning on smoking.

Flavia Carlos yanks out both her eyes from her face and skewers them on the cigarette holder, then she proceeds to barbeque them over the cigarette lighter fire.

When her eyes are bubbling and sputtering and dripping scalding vitreous fluid, she removes them from the flame and offers them to you.

"Eat up, my love," she says, "These are the windows to my soul. Love only me."

Teething Troubles

Kelly says I should blog this just in case someone else has the same experience we did. It concerns what happened with our third kid, our son Jake.

Now if you've had kids before, you'll be familiar with the pattern: they eat and sleep and eat and sleep till they're about nine or ten months old, when they become irritable and feverish. And then they start really defecating too.

At that time you know it's time for them to have their teeth, right?

We had no problem with our first two kids. Once it got to the eight month, we sent off the standard reminder email to World Inc. and waited. They delivered bang on time, almost like they'd a timer telling them exactly when the kid's irritation level would start rising. Maybe they do.

Anyhow, with Jake we sent off the request for his teeth and waited; only they didn't come. At first we thought it was simply an oversight, our email getting accidentally deleted, so we sent off another email, and waited a bit more.

Still no teeth arriving in the mail, no.

By this time we were both tired of changing baby Jake's diapers. Each new defecation seemed to shrill: "I want my teeth, where are they!?"

It was the stink that really made us finally call World Inc. Customer Care. You see the thing is, along with the teeth they send the teething powder, and that helps stop the endless toileting.

"We've been waiting for close to a month now for delivery of our son's teeth," Kelly said heatedly to the lady who appeared onscreen. "We've sent in two emails so far, but still no reply . . . the smell in our house is becoming unbearable."

"It's unusual for our . . ." Then she seemed to have an understanding of some sort. "Your names please?"

"Mr. and Mrs. Mark Davidson."

She tapped her keyboard for a few seconds, studied her computer screen, then returned her attention to us. She was smiling.

"No problem at all," she said. "You've simply got one of the new models of child."

Kelly and I stared at her in incomprehension. She explained:

"The teeth are already built into your child's jaws. You just need to manually adjust the screws to release them. Doing so also releases teething hormones to stop the irritability and fever. It's a simple procedure, explained in detail in the manual which came with your son."

Kelly managed to nod and hang up, then we sat staring at each other for about an hour.

Considering ourselves experts in child raising, neither of us had bothered to read Jake's manual.

It was all in there, just like she'd said. It was the work of thirty minutes to unzip Jake's gums, locate his teeth screws and twist them clockwise till his milk teeth were fully exposed.

The house smelt better by the next day.

It just goes to show: always read the manual.

Jackie Chan Angel

You're stopped on Sunset Boulevard by an angel who looks like Jackie Chan.

"Ninja Turtles?" he says, which means: "Dude, where's your damn license and registration?" His wings flap angrily behind him like they're beating you up.

You look for your papers, but then realize both that you've forgotten them at home and that you're driving your wife's car instead of yours.

You call your wife. The phone rings in the purse of one of three middle-aged women draped in the Stars and Stripes a few feet away.

The woman answers her phone: "Yes, hon?"

She's not your wife, but it occurs to you that she'll do for now. "I need you to talk to the cops, dear."

You put the phone on speaker.

"Ninja Turtles?" Jackie Chan Angel says.

"It's because the thanksgiving turkey was overdone," the Stars-and-Stripes woman replies.

You somehow know her response has gotten you into big trouble.

Jackie Chan Angel arrests you. Unable to fit his wings into your car, he pulls them off and glues them onto the hood. They make fantastic hood ornaments.

He gets in. The three Stars-and-Stripes draped women walk over and climb into your car also.

"Hi, dear," you say to the one you're borrowing as wife for the moment.

"Shut up and drive," Jackie Chan Angel growls, breaking off a chunk of hamburger from your headrest and sharing it with the ladies in the back.

II

At the traffic lights near the police station, you hit a speed bump and your car melts down into a metallic ocean.

The three Stars-and-Stripes women take to the sky, transforming into jets launching from the deck of the aircraft carrier the USS Jackie Chan.

They circle overhead, dive-bombing you with Stars and Stripes that illuminate the night skies of your presidential inauguration.

"I pledge to uphold the constitution of the United States of America!" you cry to the faceless fish multitudes rendered homeless when the sea metallized and now gasping out their last breaths on its silver surface. "One of the priorities of my administration will be to provide low cost aquariums for all . . . free plankton for elementary schools of fish . . ."

All the fish stare back at you, rendered speechless by the legislative loopholes stuck in their throats.

Your troubles are only just beginning. The jet-women launch again from the USS Jackie Chan.

"Get that damn traitor!" one screams.

You consider your lack of political clout. Shit! If you can't be president of the USA, you can at least get away.

You turn and flee, running with all your might to escape, but your legs run heavy, as if they're dreaming.

The choking fish regard you in horror, knowing if you can't escape this mess you've made of things, no-one can.

"We're all gonna fry!" one manages to gasp.

The fish flops violently and dies, its last words ringing horribly in your ears.

In desperation, you call your wife, your _real_ wife this time, and finally get through to her.

"Ninja—"

"There's too much stuffing in the turkey!" she interrupts you angrily.

You know this means you're going to die a coward's death in a foreign country. Maybe Cuba.

You sight her—your real wife—on the deck of the USS Jackie Chan. She's dressed in an admiral's uniform, over which she's wearing an apron and pink oven gloves, and carrying a roast photograph of you.

The three middle-aged women-jets now swoop in for the final assault—exploding Stars and Stripes splash the molten flow all round you.

Then you sight Jackie Chan Angel's wings fluttering over the silver water a short distance away. You jump and grab the wing's feet with your teeth, not caring that they're bloodstained.

The wings try to shake you off, but you cling on.

"The turkey's in the oven!" you sign with your hands.

The angel wings understand this to mean 'hit warp speed for Chinese Heaven'. They soar off into the inauguration night, with you literally holding on for dear life.

Below you, the three middle-aged women peck the surface of the ocean for Abraham Lincoln clones. Then they start arguing over which of them will be Secretary of State in the new administration.

The homeless fish take refuge in their shadows, glad to be unnoticed and uneaten.

"Be home in time for dinner, dear!" Admiral Real Wife yells, waving from the deck of the USS Jackie Chan.

III

Jackie Chan Angel's wings beat powerfully, pulling you up closer and closer to Chinese Heaven.

Once there you will pray to Chinese God and after transcending yourself, return to Earth to save the fish trusting in you for deliverance.

But you're getting vertiginous.

Thankfully, you don't wake up. You pray you never will.

Ears are for Hearing

When Obi was a little boy, he was taken into the forest by the village elders and shown a little snake. It was red with blue bands, and looked asleep. It seemed harmless to Obi; he felt like squashing it beneath the soles of his feet to demonstrate his bravery to the elders.

A restraining hand prevented his show of bravado however.

"Don't go near it," the chief elder—an old, old man who Obi was sure was actually God in disguise—said nervously. *"Ears are for hearing, little one*. Kill any other snake you see when you become a hunter, but don't go near that one: that is the snake that killed your father."

This little thing? Obi was far less than impressed. He'd always looked up to his father, but now felt a great lessening of the esteem in which he'd held the late Amadi.

He understood now why the elders, before bringing him here, had sworn him to silence with an oath at the village shrine, warning him strictly, on pain of death, to keep all that he saw and discovered a secret, not telling even his mother anything. Seeing the slumbering serpent which had killed his father, Obi felt less than even Ibe, the drunkard's son.

His father had been a coward; he, Obi, would never trample that shameful route.

"When I grow old," he boasted, salvaging what little self-esteem he could, "I will kill that snake."

The elders laughed. "That is what your father said, when he was young and we told him the same thing," the god-elder said.

Still laughing, the party returned to the village.

***

17

Seasons came and went, and Obi grew up into a fine young man. He married Chinyere, one of the village's most beautiful damsels.

More seasons came and went. Obi and Chinyere had a son. Obi grudging named the boy Amadi, in respect of his late father's sullied memory.

One day little Amadi asked his father about his grandfather. Obi hummed and harrred, unable to think up a suitable reply to his son's questions.

That night, unable to sleep, he realized he had something to take care off. But, wouldn't it be too late? Would the snake still be there after all this time?

***

Early the next morning, Obi, machete slung meaningfully over his back, made his way into the forest. He navigated by imagining he was a child again, wondrously accompanying the elders through the twisting and turnings of the almost-invisible path through the trees.

***

The snake was there like Obi remembered it from childhood, asleep in the mud the night's rain had made of the forest floor. Staring at it, Obi felt all the shame of fielding his little son's questions of the previous day pile on him. The feeling that his father Amadi hadn't been man enough threatened to topple him like a wrestler.

"For our family honor, father!" he screamed, lopping off the snake's head with a single violent blow.

For a moment he was surprised; he'd expected the tormentor of his ego to put up resistance, to be harder to kill.

Then the earth he stood on split, the grass parting like lips.

Before Obi could understand what was happening, the ground beneath his feet had opened up into a huge, huge mouth; a mouth lined with rows and rows of horribly large teeth which descended into a red pit with bubbling slimy walls.

Obi dropped straight into it.

He screamed and fought, first to escape, then to free himself, hacking at the closing jaws to no avail. As he was slowly shredded into chunks by the ground-beast's chewing, he understood that his father hadn't been the coward he thought he'd been.

Dying in a horror he'd never imagined existed, he realized also, that ears *are* for hearing.

***

Finally the ground-beast was done eating Obi. It spat up his right hand, which it found unpalatable on account of the machete Obi had refused to let go of even while dying. It extruded a long tongue and licked its grass-lips clean of Obi's blood. Then it burped, a loud sound that reached Obi's village, and made the god-elder smile. It retracted its tongue and shut again.

Above it, with the ground once again innocent-looking, its snake feeler grew out another head. The old one had somehow rolled over to Obi's severed hand and clamped its jaws into its wrist.

***

Obi was buried with the highest honors the village could afford. True, he wasn't awarded the posthumous chieftaincy title Chinyere wanted, but still, she was satisfied that all her friends (though not willing to part with their husbands just yet) envied her. For years afterwards, angry women provoked their husbands by calling them cowards, not man enough to die wrestling a lion to save the village from danger, like Chinyere's husband had.

***

The village elders smiled secret satisfied smiles as they led Obi's son Amadi through the forest. Things had gone as planned: Apaaadi the ground-beast would sleep soundly for another generation, sleep until it was sacrifice time again.

They reached the spot where Obi had been eaten by Apaaadi. The god-elder (little Amadi thought he looked like God's elder brother) pointed:

"Little one, this is the snake that killed your father. *Ears are for hearing.* When you become a hunter, you may hunt and kill any beast in the forest, but not this one."

This little thing? Amadi thought scornfully, already feeling disgust for his father's lack of manliness. He laughed. "I am still a small child," he said, "but when I grow up, I will kill this snake."

The elders laughed also in return.

"That is what your father said also, when he was young and we told him the same thing," the god-elder said.

Still laughing, with little Amadi boasting of what's he'd do to the ground-beast's snake-feeler when he was an adult, the party returned to the village.

Evil Beef Factory

I

You spot the power flower two moments before it spots you. Startled, it twitters at you, puffing its petals like it's about venomizing your eyes.

You fire at it. It turns and skitters off, its ten insect legs tapping the floor like it's Fred Astaire.

You dash after the little bastard.

The power flower ducks into an alley. You duck in after it, then realize your mistake.

It's a android trap.

"That's far enough, Doc," a mech says, stepping in front of you. Four others surround you, meat cleavers raised like you're their favorite Christmas roast.

"Hand the gun over nice and slow, Doc," the android says. "Don't try anything heroic; Mrs. wants you alive."

You ignore its advice. You raise your gun to shoot it, then slump to the floor, knocked senseless by a cleaver butt.

II

When you awake, the lower half of your body's been replaced by a brown and white piebald cow.

Damn.

In addition, your right arm's now a plasteel tank muzzle.

"Not bad," Mrs. says, entering. "Not bad at all—you look like a 60s acid trip."

You grimace. Mrs. looks like Marlene Dietrich, sexy cool as ice. Originally from North Texas, she speaks with a pronounced drawl you always mentally surf over.

She's a *real odd* cookie.

Her dad was a Baptist minister. The old guy was so exacting, Mrs. vowed to do everything bad possible to ensure she'd go to Hell, to make certain she'd be as far away as possible from him in the afterlife.

Mrs. is so hung-up she's glorious—her TOTAL inability to have an orgasm is the least of her complexes/issues.

"What do you want?" you ask while an android milks the cow you're attached to.

"Gotta job for you. Simple. You're running an errand to EBF for me."

"Oh no you don't . . ." you protest. "Count me friggin out of . . ."

She emo-rapes you, in five seconds rewinding you through the nightmare of your six-year-long marriage to Grace Kelly.

"Don't get me started on you," she says. "Without even remembering I'm doing it, I can endlessly fast forward and rewind you through bad relationships for the next five years."

(Like an NGO, Mrs. thrives on misery. Androids flock to her like bees to pollen—the andys are sickos, mechanical junkies tripping on bad vibes. To them, Mrs. is the emotional mother lode.)

"I'll go," you whimper, your feelings now splattered worse than a dragonfly meeting a windshield. "Just don't fuck my mind again."

You go.

III

At this end of the rainbow the sky looks like a split watermelon, the clouds its brown seeds.

"She's married to herself."

"Huh? Who?"

"Mrs.," your cow underbody answers. "She's married to herself," it repeats. "You ever hear of her mister?"

"Shut up," you whisper.

You're not being nasty—you're entranced by EBF.

EBF—Evil Beef Factory—is a six-story-high cube built of side-stacked cows, some skinned and alive, most dead.

It smells like six hundred gutters full of decayed rats.

Your bovine underbody falls to its four knees in worship, udders spurting milk like it's lactose-incontinent.

"HOLY COW!!" it moans. "HALLELUYAH!!!"

You forget it for the moment.

The cow-building facing you opens ninety-six alligator-yellow eyes and blinks them in sections like banks of floodlights.

"Mrs. sent me," you say.

"Who *are* you?" Its voice is an ominous lowing transmitted simultaneously from the throats of the hundred animals closest to you.

"Dr. Adrian Forever," you reply. "I clean up shit when the shit's owners don't want to wipe their own asses."

EBF considers. "You ever shoot clay pigeons?"

You indicate your tank-cannon right arm. "Olympic silver medalist," you lie.

"Good. Need you to kill some pesky gators."

You prod your undercow upright. "Get up, church is over."

IV

Openings open in EBF's walls. Circus cannons are wheeled out by clowns to leather ledges.

The cannons fire at you, filling the sky with alligators wearing crash helmets and doing aeronautics.

"Shoot to kill," Evil Beef Factory moos at you. "Or *be* killed."

You raise your weapon arm and start shooting, blasting alligators to bits in midair like they're fucking clay and you're a living shotgun.

The reptile gore doesn't fall to earth however. It sticks to the sky, like the air is a windshield.

You don't realize you've missed killing a couple of alligators till sudden pain rips through your missing legs.

Looking down, you find two allied gators—one British and one French—have severed your cow's head and are fighting over it.

You blast both out of their misery, then, ignoring the pain from your cow-neck-stump, now spurting blood like you're ejaculating red cum, you resume blowing the allies out of the air.

Seeing reptilia fails to overcome you, the allied alligators transmute to metal and bombard you with relief packages.

Realizing you've realized you've been tricked, Evil Beef Factory sends out reinforcements.

Waves of androids swarm the space separating you whilst you're repulsing the allies.

The mechs can't reach you however. They bog down in the blood/milk river flowing from you. Occasionally you turn your attention to them, blowing them away like they're skittles in a bowling alley.

Mrs. marches out of EBF. She's carrying a white truce flag with a painting of a cow fellating a cowboy on it.

"Lunch declares a ceasefire," she says.

"Fair enough," you spit at her, "but wipe the alligators off my windshield sky. I've places to be."

The androids rush to comply. When the sky is clear of allied blood and guts, and you can see the highway clearly, you smile at Mrs..

She gets into your car. The androids load Evil Beef Factory, now suitcase-sized, into the trunk.

"Wanna catch a movie?" Mrs. a.k.a. Marlene Dietrich asks. "I could *really* get divorced from myself on the way."

You nod. Feeling like Clark Gable, you drive across stage into the sunset.

Angie Stone's Revival

Angie Stone woke up in a cold wood box. It was dark and damp and underground.

It took her quite a while to splinter the box top and dig herself out. Thankfully her nails had grown long and hard in the time she'd been asleep, so that helped her dig faster.

Once outside in the shadow of the moon she realized she was wearing her wedding dress, only it was ragged like the moths had gotten to it.

She dusted herself down, headed for home.

Last thing she could remember was going into Mauricio's den. Drug bust—six kilos of uncut coke just arrived from Paraguay. (Angie hadn't called for backup. She was tired of her male partners taking all the credit for her legwork.)

She remembered seeing Mauricio's gun pointing at her face like it was an eye examining her for fear, then lightning flashing from it, then . . . nothing.

She became aware of the wind blowing through her forehead, and examined both the entrance and exit point of the bullet, small hole in front, huge crater rear opposite.

She shrugged. She felt okay, so that was okay. A little skull air-conditioning would prevent her being so hot-headed in future.

***

Angie got home to the trailer she shared with her boyfriend Terry.

Butch Bulldog saw her and ran to meet/greet her, yelping and dancing with joy.

Angie realized she still liked Butch Bulldog, just not like before. Besides, the walk from her bedroom in the cemetery had made her hungry.

She bent and cuddled the frisky bulldog, then ripped out its throat with her teeth, which had also grown long and strong while she'd been asleep.

Butch kicked, whimpered and thrashed a bit, but soon quieted down so she could eat him.

Angie ate as much of Butch as she could, till chunks of its meat starting spilling through the rot holes in her belly. Then she abandoned the dog's remains and walked over to the trailer.

***

She climbed in through an open window, something she'd warned Terry about forever, to no avail.

Except for the mess, home was much as she remembered it. TV, sofa, table littered with old pizza boxes and copies of Sports Illustrated.

Wow, the Lakers won the playoffs again, Terry must be incensed. Angie shrugged; she'd told him forever to stop supporting the Boston Celts.

One corner of the living room space was now a shrine dedicated to beer. Empty cans were stacked knee high, obliterating all signs of the trash box which had once received them. What the . . . ?

With the state of the place, one would have thought Terry was in mourning.

Angie's thoughts shifted to little Tim. Her baby, her lovely baby son. She padded into his room.

Like the living room, It hadn't been cleaned in a long while. Used feeding bottles were piled in a corner, like Terry thought they could be returned to the store for a refund.

Ah, Terry. Through the walls she could hear his loud boozy snoring.

Tim was gurgling in his bassinet. He smiled in confusion at Angie.

"Oooh, babykins," Angie said. "Mummy's back home now. You'll be fine."

Her voice somehow came out all wrong, like slowed-down music.

Tim started crying 'cos of the strange noise.

Angie misinterpreted the reason why. "Ooh, my darling Timmykins is hungry is he?" she cooed at him.

She picked Tim up to pacify him, baring her left breast and sticking it into his mouth.

This Tim could understand. He began savaging the nipple like he was making up for lost time. Then he removed his mouth from the nipple and growled his frustration.

Angie understood that her milk had run dry while she'd been asleep. She considered mixing some formula for him, then thought better of it; the health services all agreed breastfeeding was best.

Instead, she got a knife from the kitchen and sliced off her left nipple. She put the nipple where she could retrieve it later.

She then squeezed her breast till a little fatty tissue mixed with blood ooze came out of the hole, and fed that to Tim, who sucked it in like he couldn't tell the difference.

"See now, babykins, mumsy wumsies here to . . ."

She stopped singing to Tim on noticing he'd turned pale. Tim turned transparent, till he was made of glass.

Angie was so shocked, she dropped him. She was much more shocked when Tim shattered to bits on the trailer floor.

Angie stared at her son's fragments for two minutes, then, mourning over, she left his nursery, taking care not to cut her bony feet on any of the sharp glass shards Tim had become.

***

What the hell? Angie thought, peering in at the piled, unwashed plates in the kitchenette sink, this is too fucking much. *I've been gone for how long* . . . Here Angie's thoughts hit a mental wall; she didn't know how long it had been since Mauricio had shot her and she'd fallen asleep, and now . . .

Angry, she went to confront Terry about the mess in their home.

***

Terry was in their bed, naked on his back and snoring.

Angie's anger left her immediately she saw he had a boner, a meat flagpole with a mushroom head. It felt like . . . *ages* since they'd . . . fucked.

She removed her tattered dress and got her bottle of KY from her dresser. After a liberal application to her cunt, she climbed on the bed and squatted over him, carefully guiding his cock into herself.

"Ah, baby, that's so good," she moaned, sliding up and down his erection.

She fucked Terry *extra* hard. So hard chunks of Butch Bulldog squirted out of the rot holes in her belly.

No bother, there was still half of the dog left.

Terry didn't wake up all the while she fucked him.

She came, then collapsed on his chest.

"Oh God, yessssss!" she groaned. This was absolutely her greatest damn come ever.

"Hey, wake up, sleepy!" she growl-giggled at Terry in her afterglow slow-mo voice. "I'm back home."

Terry didn't respond. Angie discovered he'd been turned to glass, just like Tim.

She climbed off him, glad to see he still had a glass boner.

I'll fuck more, eat more, later, she thought.

Now, however, there was work to be done.

A glance at the wall clock showed her it was 1 a.m. Angie knew most criminals would just now be getting warmed up for the night's illegal activities.

She opened her side of their wardrobe. Her cop uniform still hung there, neatly pressed like she'd left it.

She put it on, then loaded and strapped on her spare pistol.

She examined herself in the mirror.

She did look rather pale. Nothing a little makeup wouldn't fix though.

Angie Stone sat down at the dresser and made up her face. It took awhile, both because she was out of practice and because her nails had grown so long, but finally she got her look together.

Yeah, that's better, she thought, enjoying this new version of herself. Red lips, lime-green eye shadow, blush . . .

Her uniform smelt of mothballs so she doused herself with Chanel No. 5.

Angie winced at the holes in her head, how she could see clean through her skull's reflection out the reflected bedroom window. She shrugged; it couldn't be helped.

After a final look at glass-Terry lying rigid in bed, boner cocked like a gun about to fire, reanimated Detective Sergeant Angie Stone left the house to resume her efforts policing DC's crime. In particular she intended visiting that drug-dealing Paraguayan shithead Mauricio and explaining to him why one didn't go around shooting hardworking policewomen in the head.

She made a mental note to also stop at an all-nighter for some superglue, and to ask where she could buy instructions for re-assembling a shattered glass child. She couldn't just leave little Tim lying around the floor in bits now, could she?

That would be asshole parenting.

Lesbian in my Pocket

A friend of mine named Richard has a lesbian named Ellen where his penis used to be.

His lesbian used to live in his pocket, coming out only occasionally to snatch his girlfriends, but now, by mutual agreement, she's migrated to his crotch and taken over his sexual functions completely.

Like Richard, she's life-sized.

Their arrangement works something like this:

During the day, when they go to work, Richard tucks Ellen away between his legs. Folded up like that, she maintains for him the illusion that he still possesses a penis.

At night, however, when they go clubbing, at the first sight of a beautiful woman Ellen tucks Richard away between her buttocks (actually up her anus), so they can chat her up.

Living like this, Richard now seems to have a more satisfactory sex life than the rest of us, his friends.

So now we're all thinking of getting lesbians of our own to replace our penises.

Void

The bus was halfway across the bridge when the helicopter landed in front of it.

In a scene ripped from a spy movie, the burnt-metal craft first overtook, then flew ahead of them for a hundred meters, finally circling and landing. Its three propellers slowed, but not to a halt.

Unable to navigate around it, the bus slowed and stopped.

Seated at the bus's rear, Jenny Loveless—disguised as a wrinkled old woman, the load of money she'd stolen from Bender strapped in a belt around her waist—watched the helicopter land with misgivings. She suspected they were either looking for her, or the girl seated next to her.

The pimply redhead beside her seemed almost as worried as she was. Jenny knew her name was Void—she'd seen her sign it at the bus station.

She'd first thought Void a drughead, but now wasn't sure. Something about the dreamy look in her eyes and the way she spoke said she was more than she appeared to be. And once, when Void had brushed her hair aside to scratch behind her ear, Jenny had seen the socket.

Brainbolt. The sort governments put in their mutants to keep them under control. Void's socket was a deep pit filled with angry red scar tissue. Her 'plug' had clearly only recently been removed.

And that forcibly.

***

Jenny saw the brighter-than-real-life coloration, the thick black outline of the individual stepping first onto the bus, and groaned audibly.

Fuck no.

It was Cart Jack, Bender's number one assassin—a psychotic animation. Being a cartoon meant Cart had simply ridiculous powers of regeneration. No matter how hard you blew him up, shredded him, or filled him with bullet holes, he'd be as good as new in ten seconds. Jenny had once witnessed Cart get burnt to ashes in a car crash; then she'd witnessed him 'unburn'—being restored to normal again like he was a video playing backwards.

She didn't know the other four with him. All were cartoons however—black and white drawings of sunglassed men in pinstriped suits carrying ultra-large guns.

***

"We're not here to hurt anyone. We're simply looking for a thieving tranny bitch." Cart laughed, revealing huge donkey teeth. "I guess that lets all the guys off—she wouldn't have had time to lose her tits. Nah . . . undo your shirts anyway. But girls—a little make-up and . . ." He laughed louder. "Here's what we're doin' ladies. Each of you will be so kind as to pull down your pants and spread your legs."

I'm fucked, Jenny thought desperately. *No way in hell I'm getting out of this alive.* Beside her Void rocked gently, softly humming an atonality that gave Jenny the creeps.

The frontmost seated of the women in the bus were already complying with the directive to bare themselves. Once bare-bummed they bent over, were examined, and given the nod by Cart to pull their pants back up.

Jenny was unarmed; guns were forbidden on the bus, not that having one would make much difference against the toons.

She turned to whisper in Void's ear. "It's *you* they've come for, young woman," she said.

Void turned to her in horror. "Not me, grandma. They're looking for a *transsexual.*"

"Void, do those guys look like they make a habit of telling the truth?"

"*How* . . . how do you know my name?"

"I'm psychic," Jenny lied smoothly, keeping the desperation out of her voice. "On my way to do a show in Heaventown." She peered intently into the girl's face. "You have to use your powers to defend yourself; else they'll take you back and plug you in again."

She saw she'd been right. The dreaminess in Void's eyes gave way to *something* else. Suddenly Jenny was *very* scared. Some muties were really powerful; she had no idea what this one could do—if maybe she *wasn't* better locked away.

"But I shouldn't . . . I'm bad . . ." Void whimpered. Then her face hardened. "I'm not going back there, grandma. You have no idea what it was like, what they—"

Cart noticed them. "Hey! Shut up back there!" He extended his right arm till it was four times the length of his body, and wagged his index finger in their faces. "We'll get to you—"

"No!" Void screamed. "Nooooo! I'm not going back there! Neverrrrr!!!"

***

Existence visibly distorted—like someone had crushed a soft drink can—then straightened out again. Things looked *almost* normal once more.

Only now, the front three-quarters of the bus was missing. As was a large portion of the bridge ahead of them, including that on which the helicopter had been parked.

There was a jarring thud as the bus's undercarriage, now lacking its front suspension, hit the road hard.

Like the bus itself, the four passengers seated at the shearing point had been sliced vertically in two. Two of the new half-corpses, displaced by the sudden jerk, fell forward and out of their seats—down out of sight.

The woman behind one of them began crying, two others started screaming. The reek of fear was so bad, Jenny was sure people were peeing their pants.

Cart Jack and the toon goons were all gone too.

Jenny stared at the truncated remains of the bus and bridge in horror. "Shit, girl, what did you just do!?"

"I got rid of them," Void replied dreamily. "They can't hurt me now. Or anyone else."

33

"You're *dead* right about that."

***

A hundred feet below, the dragon-infested Unan wastelands stretched out interminably; ahead was empty space for a hundred meters then the bridge began again; above was blue sky with red and green clouds. Looked like rain.

Behind them the bridge still existed.

"Well c'mon, Void," Jenny said, preparing to climb out of the rear window. She'd coldly decided the girl was good protection to have around. "If we can't go forward, we can always go back."

Can't See For The Rain

It's been raining eyes for six weeks now. *Human* eyes. They're everywhere, black eyes, blue eyes, red eyes, yellow eyes, pink, brown, green and purple eyes; albino eyes even. Sort of like hail, but softer.

At first it was a major inconvenience, having to avoid them—if stomped they become this gooey pulp which is harder to get off shoes than schoolgirl-chewed gum.

Then a new company 'Demonpharm' (am I the only one who finds their name less than confidence-inspiring?) made a twofold discovery: First, a painless eye-transplant procedure, and second, that it worked on the falling eyes.

What happened next? Yeah, you guessed right. With eyes raining all over the world (except over Beijing for some reason), everyone rushed for the new procedure, ditching their original eyes for new ones. It's ongoing too—most people I know change eyes at least once a week.

(This last is encouraged by the government. The worst thing the government's done so far in my opinion is the weekly 'eyepop' events, you know where people dispose of their 'old' eyes into huge mobile bonfire furnaces. The 'eyepop' monicker came about because it sounds like they're making 'eye popcorn' when they burst.

The government says eyepopping was introduced to stimulate the 'eyeconomy'—huge eye turnover equals huge eye taxes on Demonpharm.

The government's dumb as a carrot, But what can you expect from a Rabbit parliament? The president's a Bug, the prime minister a Bunny. I know that sounds like a scene from a children's cartoon but it's not even half as funny.)

There've been three eye-trends so far. First, it was having eyes of different colors, then it was 'eyeball' eyes (you know the kind the undead slasher has in scary movies—all white without iris or pupils), and now, it's *eye-shades*, where the left and right eyes are the same color, only one is a lighter shade than the other, so you get a disorienting 'traveling' feeling of motion when you look at whoever's face.

Now I'm not an eyelier-than-thou religious hypocrite; I'm not immune to fads myself.

While I avoided the first two, eye-shades has sort of won me over. They look cool, if you avoid the girly colors and get with the 'gangster' look. I'm currently on my sixth set of 'shades' now—my left one is black, the right a water-transparent middle tone of grey. Gives me great pep when I've to deal with recalcitrant customers.

Yesterday Demonpharm announced *eye-shadow*, a new eyedrop which alters the color of the eyes you've already got, without you taking them out first. They say it's their response to customer requests for cost-saving measures, though with eyes as plentiful as sand everywhere, and replacement costs as low as subway fares, who're they fooling?

More relevant and interesting (if you've a high pain threshold), they also recently patented the *eyejection*, an eyeball hypodermic that enables you color your eye's orb different from its iris . . . and from each other.

My girlfriend Briss is really into this, with her freaky Asian dominatrix thing. Her right eye is currently blue and yellow and her left one red and black. (Yes, she is a sight for sore eyes . . . ha ha . . . sorry, couldn't resist the urge.)

(Her name's actually Bliss, but . . . well let's say I never put much stock into Chinese 'r' and 'l' vocal switchover stereotyping until we started dating.)

And still eyes keep raining. Everywhere in the world that isn't Beijing, rain clouds fill the sky like they're going to pour water on people and pour out eyes instead.

***

So on Earth now we've eyes to spare. Which should be good, shouldn't it?

But I've got a sneaky feeling about all this—A BAD feeling. I'm certain we're all going to wake up one morning and find that these new eyes cause cancer or they'll turn into water in our faces, and . . . and . . . something much, much worse . . .

(And if you think them turning into water sounds far-fetched, remember I just said they fall out of *rain* clouds?)

***

Just after the Demonpharm eye-rush began, I asked Briss: "Briss honey, why eyes never fall over Beijing?" (She'd just come over, her English wasn't too good.)

"Chinese see flar ahead," she replied while buckling on her thigh-length orange leather boots. "Rong civirization, rong histoly of lead and pran future. We not need flesh eyes."

"But *you're* using them."

"Because I lesident in decadent capitarist county," she retorted, putting in her cockroach-strung nose rings. She waited till she'd hung on her (life-sized but hollow) tuna earrings before adding angrily: "You know I cultural-exchange student; if I exchange eye as wer I leplesenting Chinese intlests."

I saw she was angry with me, tried to kiss her. She pushed me off, glared freshly transplanted red orbs at me. "Keep decadent capitarist hands away flom rovery sociarist body."

And to make her point she draped her live-toad cloak over the 'rovery sociarist body' in question. She glared some more at me, her cloak-toads rolled their eyes and wagged disapproving tongues at me.

Watching her/them walk off, I realized I love her because she makes me look much less mundane and boring.

But her comments stuck with me. And lomance . . . sorry I mean *romance*, aside, she sounds more and more like a spy every day.

So unlike everyone else I know, I was smart enough not to get taken in by all the 'eye popcorn' nonsense.

Unknown even to my darling Briss, I've kept my original eyes in a pickle jar in the fridge, so I'll know exactly where they are when the rain stops, our new eyes all dissolve—running liquid from their sockets—and the Chinese invasion begins.

Identia

Your phone rings. It's Herr Bormann.

"A job for you, Identia," he says in his Germanic tones.

"What sort?"

"A killing; make it look like an accident."

"And my disguise?" you ask.

"The courier is outside your door now." He hangs up.

You open the door and let the courier in. This time it's a middle-aged man in red latex bondage gear. You take him upstairs and whip him for an hour as payment, then kick him out.

You now open the suitcase he brought. It contains a bloody severed Asian woman's head, a pair of arms, two breast implants, a blue silk cheongsam dress and gold slippers, and a set of instructions.

You read your instructions. Today you are Shan Wu, wife of Dr. Fu-han Wu, the geneticist. You are to kill your husband.

You head for the basement.

Switching heads is *always* painful. It's like being raped. You *know* this from experience: you once arranged to be raped, just so you could compare notes.

Your doctor demon is however the best. It decapitates and repairs you in under a minute, so you don't feel violated too long.

Soon you're seeing through Shan Wu's dead eyes. You admire the seamless join of your new head and neck.

Next, the doctor demon chops your arms off at the shoulders and attaches Shan's in their place. Then it replaces your breast implants with her smaller ones.

You head for the bathroom to wash the blood off.

Once cleaned up, you dress in the supplied cheongsam and pretty yourself up.

It's Shan Wu's birthday today. Dr. Wu is treating his wife to a private celebratory dinner at Club Tang in Chinatown.

You smile. You're hungry now. Besides, murder always feels better on a full stomach.

The Morning After

There's a wheeled man outside," Mrs. Blunt said.

It was true: On opening the door, I looked in the street and there he was. It was Michael. He was lying flat on his back, his arms bound to his sides by metal strips. But that wasn't the worst. Sticking out of his chest was a huge motor engine, the sort with exhaust tubes on both sides—I still have no idea how it had been grafted into place. It huffed and puffed like the big bad wolf, huffed and puffed, blowing clouds of smoke up at me.

He had two axles, one somehow forced through his shoulders; the other through his ankles. Large wheels now supported his upper body, small ones the lower. His body itself was as rigid as if it now had steel supports running through it. I shook in horror; someone had done Michael up like he was a Formula One race car.

Odd thing was: he wasn't bleeding anywhere. In addition, all I'm now describing looked eerily natural, like I'd somehow translocated a dream image into reality.

"Hi, Jake," he said brightly as I stared speechless, "I spent last night with Marie. It was *fantastic*." His voice had the high pitch of someone about to have a nervous breakdown. As he spoke, motor oil leaked from his nostrils.

I managed to find my voice. "Have you looked in the mirror today?" Even as I spoke the stupidity of the question impressed itself on me.

"Why? I feel great—better than I ever have before. Well, I've got to be going now. Marie insisted I be back in time for lunch; she's rather touchy about tardiness."

While I gaped in total incomprehension, he rolled off into the distance.

Ahmed Apple Attacks America!

Adam ate Amy's almonds.

Angry at aforementioned abusive appropriation, Amy abducted Adam and aimed an agonizing assault at Adam's arms and associated appendages.

Adam anguished at Amy's animus.

"Ahm appalled, Adam!" Amy asserted, "at an adult's actions akin an animal's!"

"Ambrosial almonds art an addiction," afflicted Adam answered authentically.

"Ass!" Amy asserted angrily, applying additional agony. "Asinine ass."

Ahmed Arrives

An AK-47 armed apple approached Amy and Adam.

"Ahm Ahmed Apple," apple acquainted. "Ahm against anyone and anything American. An awful American ate Aunt Agnes."

Adam angrily advanced at Ahmed Apple.

"Ahm American, applejuice, and ah ain't afraid—"

Ahmed Apple assassinated Adam, aiming AK-47 at Adam's arrogant ass. "Ah ain't an amusement arcade act!" Ahmed angrily asserted.

Anger amplified, Ahmed aimed AK-47 at Amy also. "And . . . ?" Ahmed asked aggressively.

"Ahm Afghanistani," an anxious Amy answered. "Ah absolutely abhor America."

41

Ahmed's Army and Allies, Assault and Attack Approach

Against America, Ahmed Apple allied alongside Australia, Austrian athletes, Afghanistan, appalled antisocial Africans, and also angry Anglo-American Atheists.

Another attack axis also assembled: Argentinians and anorexic Asian ambulance attendants, Andorrans, Algerians, alcoholic Angolans, anteaters, and affrighted Andromedian aliens.

"At arms, assaulters!" Ahmed asserted, "America's apocalypse awaits all!"

***

Ahmed's army alighted Alitalia airlines at Angeles airport.

"Advance!" Ahmed adjured. "Acquire all argent articles, automobiles, and accommodations."

Ahmed's aircraft attacked America after aligning along an Atlantic axis.

Ahmed's artillery annihilated Atlanta, Alaska, and Alabama. Airborne anchovy assaults annihilated Augusta and Albany. Apricot airmen assassinated Alitalia's airline advertisers. Ahmed also aikido-ed all absinthe-addled authors and also alcoholic academics and administrators.

America's Anti-Ahmed Action

American airships attacked Ahmed, airdropping autogenic acids against Ahmed's army. American asses also assailed Ahmed's abominable allies, attractive 'adult' actress' above-average ass-apertures anally asphyxiating all around.

America's ants also ate Ahmed's attacking anteaters.

Antithesis

At Andover Avenue, aboard an armed automobile approaching Abilene airstrip, Ahmed's Anti-Americans again accosted Amy.

"Away, Amy!" Ahmed Apple admonished, "Allez! Allez!!"

"Ah ain't afraid anymore!" Amy answered angrily. Adding: "And ahm American also, asshole!"

Ahmed addressed Abdullah, an Assegai-armed Angolan accountant. "Arrest Amy!"

Abdullah attempted and abandoned an abortive arrest, after Amy angrily Aikido-ed Abdullah's African ass.

Abdullah ached audibly away.

Ahmed's adjutant, alluring Australian artist Angela Armstrong, also attempted arresting Amy. Angela adopted an alternative arrest approach, attacking at ambush around Amy's angular anatomy.

After an anguished abbreviated attempt, an ankle-aching Angela also abandoned arresting Amy.

Alarmed, Ahmed Apple assumed Antichrist attack attitude. "Ah'll absolutely annihilate all Americans!" Ahmed avowed again.

Amy automatically altered—assuming anthropoid alias, Ape-Amy.

"Applehead Arab!" annoyed Ape-Amy also announced aggressively. "Ahm annihilating all anti-Americans."

Ahmed's Agonized Adieu

Accelerating abruptly, Ape-Amy attacked, apprehended, and ate all Ahmed's army, artillery, airplanes, and anchovy airmen.

Assailed also, Amy's ape-armor absorbed all armed, artillery, and airborne assaults, and Amy afterwards appeared as able as antecedently.

Ahmed Apple's appalled as all allied accomplices are assimilated as aliment.

Agitated, Ahmed aims AK-47 at Amy's ass.

"Ah'll accomplish all ah've . . . Arrrgh!"

Amy ate Ahmed's aiming arm, AK-47, and ammunition.

Afterward, Amy ate Ahmed Apple also.

"Alas! Alas!" an ailing and anemic Ahmed accursed aloud and anxiously. "Ahm abandoned and all alone! Ah apologize! Ah apologize!!"

Ape-Amy's awfully amused. "Antagonistic Assholes After Amnesty? Absolutely absurd!"

***

As Ape-Amy's abyssal anterior alimentary aperture absorbed Ahmed, attractive Australian adjutant Angela Armstrong absconded abroad alongside Ahmed's accountant Abdullah, alighting at Accra airport and alleging African ancestry.

Also accompanying Abdullah and Angela, are all Ahmed's arrogated/appropriated/abstracted agricultural accounts.

And as Amy's anthropoid alias abases Ahmed Apple and allied assholes, Anti-American attacks abate. Ahmed's appalling aims and anathaemic atrocities aren't achievable anymore. All anarchists, antichrists, and arsonists along an Atlantic ambit and antipodal Artic-Antarctic axis are accidented, abrogated, and aggressively arrested.

(As an aside: all arrested attackers are arraigned. Although afterwards, apathetic avaricious American attorneys accept amortizations and advance alleviating asshole arguments aimed at absolving all aggressors, alleging America aetiologically aroused Ahmed's attack.)

Afterwards, Afterword, and Aftermath: Amy's Ascent

Aim accomplished, an Andromedan alien artifact alighted and allowed Ape-Amy aboard. Ape-Amy ascended aloft, aegis apparent, although alert and aggressive at all approaching after-attackers.

Ape-Amy altered—again Amy appeared.

Amazed, awed and alive Americans ardently acclaimed and applauded Amy.

"AMY! AMY!! AMY!!!"

"Aw . . . ahm an arcane American agent," Amy admitted afterwards, appreciative and abashed, "and ah approve aur American approach."

A-nd

The Grass

During a fight, two elephants killed some grass. When the grass got to Heaven it complained to God about the nature of its demise. But to its surprise and great disappointment, God only laughed.

"Ah, my good grass," He said, "It is in the nature of elephants to trample on things and kill them, most notably innocent grasses like yourself. But don't worry; you will have your revenge."

"*How am* I to have my revenge?" The grass asked, wondering: "I'm already dead, and your divine resurrection doesn't apply to plants."

"Just trust me," replied the Almighty. "I'm not God for nothing. You'll have your revenge.'

The grass left God's presence not understanding what He meant, and in its lack of understanding, disappointed that the elephants would go scot free.

But two days later, both elephants were shot dead (on the same spot) by some hunters, and it was the dead grass, now dry, which was used to roast part of their meat for eating.

And the grass saw from Heaven, and was pleased and satisfied that justice had been done, and in reverence it bowed down and worshipped the great wisdom of God.

A Day at the Racists

Since becoming wealthy enough to do so without fear of embarrassing myself, I'd liked attending the horse races. Since meeting Miss Carol Chang, I'd come to love them.

Carol was a jockey, see. Mad about horses. I was mad about Carol.

I bought a horse. Sorry, ladies, it's a normal guy maneuver—pretty woman loves horses, I buy a horse, I get to meet her. Works every time.

***

I hit my head.

I was walking through the stables looking for Carol, thought I heard her call me, turned about hastily, and knocked myself half senseless on a horseshoe hung on a nail by a stable stall.

After the resulting headache subsided somewhat I became aware of voices speaking next to me.

"Yes," said a pretty mare stalled next to my horse, "humans have no taste whatsoever; I wonder what he sees in the yellow-skinned chink neo-communist bitch."

"Flat-chested slopehead slut," my horse added.

The horses were *talking?*

This was too real for me. "Did any of you just say something?" I asked politely.

The horses gaped at me in shock equal to mine. "You can *hear* us?"

"Uh huh." I made sure I had unobstructed access to the stable door in case of danger to my person.

"Okay, we'll level with you," my horse said. "We don't approve of your sniffing around that slant-eyed jade."

Marlon, my black chauffeur, came into window-view then. "Oh look, it's the jungle bunny again," another horse said. The rest laughed heartily in derision.

Horses talking was one thing, but there was something very disturbing about this now.

"Why'd you just call Marlon a 'jungle bunny'?" I asked, suddenly certain great enlightenment was about to hit me.

"He's black."

"So, why not just call him a *black man?*"

"Where's the fun in that? We're racists—we've got to insult people based on their ethnicity, or if that's in doubt, where they originate from."

"Aaaahh. You're joking of course."

"Nope, we're horses. All horses are racists—it's inborn."

"Are you sure you don't mean racers?"

"No, rac*ists*. Conjugate the verb 'to race.' Race, rac*er*, rac*ist*."

"Should be rac*est* then."

"Yes. Rac*ist*."

***

They *were* serious. I tested them.

Soon the crowd for the 4:00 race began to arrive.

"C'mon guys," I said, "you've *got* to love Mrs. Jackson's hat, just dig those natty feathers. And those shoes."

"Stupid fat-assed nigger bitch."

"*Stupid?* She's medical director of a hospital."

"So? Damn ho must have got her med degree on her back."

"Okay, how about Carlos Alberto? Check out that suit and Rolex he's wearing, and his wife's dress, just lovely."

"Spic drug-runner . . ."

"He's an investment banker!"

"Yeah, sure. His greasy ass came over the border hidden in a fruit-cart. I know so for sure—my cousin Dinky pulled it. And that wife of his? Good Lord, don't Mexican women *ever* stop eating?"

A distinguished old Jewish couple were crossing the lawn towards the stands. The 4:30 race would begin in fifteen minutes. I pointed them out. "And the Goldsteins?"

"I thought you had some class, boss. Please don't foul the air of this place by mentioning kikes."

***

They went on and on and on and on.

Greeks and Canadians were degenerate sodomists. Italians were all Dago Mafiosos. Australians all had kangaroo mothers. Blacks were uneducated lazy pimps and wife beaters. The French were frogs, snail eaters, and Godzilla-making nuclear degenerates.

The British? I'll have MI6 after me if I repeat what they said about the Queen and Prince Charles, the late Princess Diana, and *David Beckham*.

For some reason horses really *hate* David Beckham.

It got worse. Poor Salman Rushdie's ordeal prevents me from repeating what they said about the Shah of Iran, and Arabs in general. To the horses, terrorism was the least of the Arabs' crimes. And I think it wise not to even consider offending the Russian Mafia, the Chinese Triads, Japanese Yakuza, Africans in general—the list was almost endless.

I assure you I heard more political incorrectness in that stable than I've ever heard anywhere else in my life.

***

Finally they convinced me. I stared at the horses in horror. "You really are racists."

"Yeah, that's what we do, we race."

But you've mixed things up. There's racing and then there's . . ."

"Race, rac*er*, rac*ist*, boss."

A black stallion nodded agreement. "Word, boss."

My mind slowly wrapped itself around the concept. "Okay, so why aren't you insulting *me*? I'm Irish."

"Health insurance policy, boss. No one here wants to wind up as cans of dog food. We'll wait till you leave."

That was honest at least.

The 4:30 was over, I could see the board from the stables, Abe Goldstein's 'Golda Mare' had won.

***

I finally thought I saw where this was headed. "So, if you don't like Jews, or Blacks, or Spaniards, or Asians, or Greeks, or the British, or the Russians, or Native Americans or South Americans, or just everyday un-prefixed Americans, who *do* you like? The Germans? I mean Hitler must be your hero, right? You wanna set up the Pureblood Aryan Horse Reich?"

My horse looked at me in disgust. "Screw that damn Kraut punk and his entire country." It *groaned* at me, surprised at my hardheaded lack of comprehension of this most simple of equine principles. "We're *just* racists—*we don't discriminate.* Unlike you humans, *we dislike everyone equally.* You're *all* to blame for the state of the world.

"Worse still," the pretty mare in the next stall added, "You *all* ride on our backs."

***

Chastened, I left the stables and walked slowly back to my Rolls.

I haven't had any stomach for the racists . . . sorry I mean races, since then.

I sold my horse. It had already served its purpose. Miss Carol Chang now comes over to the house to visit me instead.

Behind Every ~~Successful~~ Woman . . .

(Author's disclaimer: Ladies this *is* a sexist tale. It isn't written for you, but for MEN, MEN, MEN. Stop reading right now, or else . . . just don't blame me afterward . . . ahem.)

As the result of humanity's losing the war with the Andromedans, all human women were stripped of their buttocks. Yes, those twin pads of fat which human men lust after were stolen by the alien fiends.

Earth's men woke up the next day feeling strangely cheated, and yet strangely at peace with themselves, as for the first time in their lives they found themselves able to stare at female members of their species without any lust whatsoever.

Even more amazing, most men now began to view women as *persons* rather than sex objects.

If men were pleased with this state of affairs, however, the female of the species most definitely wasn't.

***

Fifty miles above the Earth's surface, the ruling committee of the Female Emancipation and Domination of Man (FEm-DoM) society were deliberating what to do about this latest sex crisis.

"This is a total disaster," the goddess Electra growled, "it's almost as bad as when the feminist lobbies got equal pay for women in the workplace."

"That was *easier* to resolve," Athena interjected, "All we had to do to ensure we kept the upper hand was get the sexual harassment legislation passed through Congress."

"We're about to lose the ability to use sex as a weapon to disorient men for good, ladies," Hera said miserably. "Six thousand years of hard work is about flushing down the drain because some alien invaders . . ."

"Er . . . *mankind* started the war . . ."

"You KNOW what I mean!"

"Girls," Electra chided gently, "fighting will get us nowhere. This is way beyond any crisis we've ever faced. With the loss of buttocks, ass, tush—call it what you will, these damn Andromedans have unwittingly crippled femalekind. Of what use is it having sexes if sex can't interfere with the smooth running of society, create endless unresolvable issues, perpetually fuck up the gears of the relationship machine?"

"Yeah, *all men* love ass," Hera said reflectively.

"Gay men don't."

"Yes they do; they just love other guys' asses!"

Hera's two compatriots stared at her narrowly. "Try to be serious."

"What about trying to shift the focus from back to front, to the tits instead?"

"Won't work, it's considered sleazy to look at a woman's chest instead of her face when she's facing you. When she isn't facing you, however . . ."

"Damn, I forgot that!"

"Think, sisters, think. There has to be something men like as much as ass; all we need is to give every woman a set of those instead and the status quo is restored; ergo, we're in control again."

They deliberated on this awhile.

"Guys *love* money."

"No, cash-butts will send inflation skyrocketing."

"Cars?"

"Yes but . . . women won't be able to get through doors anymore. I like the transport concept though—keep thinking along those lines."

Finally they hit on the *perfect* solution.

***

(A brief explanation of what the FEm-DoM goddesses were so panicked about.

Despite all their protestations to the contrary, women have ALWAYS dominated men. If you've any doubts as to this, remember *accurately* your mother's relationship with your father, possibly before he left home never to return.

The average man doesn't abandon his girlfriend or wife—he flees for his life.

It makes no difference, though, as whoever they end up with, they still end up in the same place.)

***

And so it came to pass that every Earth woman now has a *motorcycle* in place of her stolen buttocks.

Things are more or less back to normal now. It's routine to hear guys ogling girls saying things like:

"Wow, dudes, check out that babe's Harley Davidson! Man, those rear lights! And those tires—just incredible!"

"That girl's a Grand Prix Honda, man."

"Nooooooo, she's a Confederate Hellcat!"

"I'll betcha five dollars."

"You guys talking bout Mary? Dudes, save your money. She's some low-cost Korean brand!"

Cocktail party conversation:

"You know, personally I'm a 16-inch rim guy myself; give me too much tire and I've no idea what to do with it."

"I know exactly what you mean. My last girlfriend was a German three-wheeler, really heavy duty, she kept leaving tracks all over my . . ."

And the ladies themselves?

"So I asked him: Do you wanna go freewheelin' sometime?"

"No you didn't, girlfriend! That's just nasty!"

"Well you know me! He looked like the sort of guy who'd be able to get a good grip on my handlebars."

"Personally I prefer a guy who fits snugly on my seat . . ."

"And you're calling *me* dirty-minded . . . ?"

And lawyers?

"Your honor, I propose to show that Mr. Mackintosh here twice attempted to oil Miss Blakeley's gears without her permission while she was working as his secretary, and also tampered with her starter-key . . ."

Fresh expressions have been coined:

"Dave's such a pain in the motorbike, Kate."

"Yeah, I know. He's a real exhaust pipe."

Teenage girls now all have either BMX bike or skateboard behinds by the way. Teenage boys are *extremely* content with those.

***

So Earth's women are happy again, no they're overjoyed, no—*ecstatic*. The man-domination business is booming better than ever before.

Earth's men, however, though happy as hell to have something to ogle and lust after and fight over again, still can't help feeling screwed.

It's like they were let off the hook for a few days, and then, just when they'd gotten used to the sweet scent of freedom—BAM! The hook's been rammed down their throats again. Only much deeper this time.

And they *still* don't understand what went wrong.

To find out, I suggest they pick another fight with the Andromedans.

Okay! Okay!!

Sam saw a picture at papercutbooks.com, and was supposed to write a story about it for a projected anthology. Weird pic. Three people, two girls and a guy, walking along a road in a resort of some kind.

The problem was—the picture meant nothing to him. If there'd been water in it maybe, but just a gravel road?

He searched desperately for inspiration; something . . . *anything*. Okay, there were some trees, one blooming—it seemed to be springtime . . .

Sam thought hard. What could he do with the trees?

***

His friend Elvis came by that afternoon. Now Elvis was dead, but no one had informed him of it yet, so he just kept on living. He was dressed in a moldy old white jump-suit and studded white leather boots. He carried an electro-acoustic guitar with long-rusted strings. The guitar was simply a prop—since dying, Elvis hadn't played a note.

He sat, cleared his throat. "Hi, Sam."

Sam hadn't noticed his entrance. "Sorry, man, got a problem— need to write a story about this bullshit photo, and I've no inspiration whatsoever."

Elvis put the guitar down, walked over and examined it. "Dumb pic, I admit; why not just write about the girls' asses? Or maybe that they're going to have sex. That'll sell for sure."

"I'm writing art, not porn." He tapped his head for a moment. "I've got it—I'll write about a love triangle. The two girls are in love with the guy—"

"Er . . ." Elvis interrupted him, "I made a mistake—the one on the left's a guy also." He pointed: "See? No bra."

Sam was unsure whether to be pleased or disgusted. "Good thing you noticed in time. Okay, so what if I reverse it? Both guys are in love with the same girl, or they're gay but she loves one . . ."

"That *might* be better . . ." Elvis began dubiously.

He never completed the statement. Two gravel-hands reached out of the bottom of the picture and pulled himself and Sam into it.

***

They found themselves in a white room. On one of its walls was the same picture Sam had been agonizing over.

On a sofa in a corner sat a female *figure* made of constantly shifting gravel.

She rose to greet them. "Welcome," she said in a gravelly voice, "my name's Granita Groundel. I couldn't help overhearing your conversa . . ." She noticed then who she'd snared. "Wow! it's the KING!!!" Her shifting pebble face creased in puzzlement. "Elvis? Man you're supposed to be . . ."

"Don't tell him!" Sam shrieked quickly.

"Don't tell me what?"

Sam surreptitiously winked at Granita. She got the message, shrugged nonchalantly. "Oh, nothing much—just that your record sales have gone through the roof since you . . ." she caught herself just in time, "did Vegas."

Elvis smiled. "Yeah, that was a *great* career move."

Sam addressed Granita. "Why'd you bring us here?"

She climbed out of her chair. Sam saw the gravel-woman had a HUGE ass.

She pointed to the wall. "I'm tired of that damn picture," she groaned. "I want you to kill the photographer for me."

***

"Why us?"

"You both were in the army. Okay, all the King did was entertain—he can drive the getaway car. You, however, were a sniper, so . . ."

"I don't get it," Elvis said as she handed Sam a rifle fitted with a telescopic sight, and himself a ring of car keys. "What's your gripe with this picture anyway?"

Granita rolled a library-style ladder up against the picture. "Shoot the bastard for me first; I'll explanation later."

Elvis juggled the keys, "I don't see no car."

"Just look in the middle, to the right; by the two *little* people next to the *large* guy's belt."

Without being sure why they were doing so, Sam and Elvis climbed the ladder and entered the picture.

Sam stared at Elvis. "Why do I get the feeling something's about to go wrong?"

***

It was. There was a corpse in the car, a neat bullet hole in its forehead.

"I think we just got framed," Elvis said, pointing to the camera draped around the dead man's neck. In the background, sirens blared.

Sam had meanwhile noticed the pair of lips in the ground beside them. "Granita?"

A gravelly hand poked out of the ground, waved to them. "Bye bye, suckers."

"Why?"

"Why!? He said I had a FAT ASS!"

Sam kept staring at the ground after Granita had melted into it.

"I think we'd best make ourselves scarce," Elvis said. He opened the driver's side door, dragged the photographer's corpse out.

"Pity he's dead," Sam said, closing the passenger door. "I'd have liked to ask him what this damn photo's about anyway."

"I've worked that out," Elvis said, starting the car.

"Huh?"

Elvis nodded. "It's about fakery."

"Huh? Don't drive so fast, you'll run into . . . Er . . . where'd those three arm-in-arm lack-of-inspirations go? Yeah . . . and all the other people?"

"That's what I'm trying to tell you. They were *never* here. The photo's a collage. You know the sort of thing you do when you're too lazy to take a *new* picture—just get bits from everywhere else and assemble them in Photoshop?"

"*Photoshop?*"

Elvis nodded. "Picture's a composite. I thought I'd seen that trio somewhere before, now I remember: they were in a Cosmo article on bisexuality."

Sam suddenly felt savage. "Let's get out of this piece of crap," he said angrily. "I feel like beating someone up. What's the name of the guy who 'chose' this photo?"

"I think his surname's Mullen." Elvis said, pumping the gas pedal so they burst out of the picture, ripping it to shreds.

Sam nodded grimly, hefting his rifle like a club. "Yeah, I remember now—*Michael* Mullen. Fuck writing anything. Let's go beat the shit out of him instead."

For Ze Love of Rosa
(A Legend of Bizarro Mexico)

I tell you ze weird story, me eses.

Rosa, she ees live in ze hut by ze river with her husband Gonzales.

Ze hut ees very small with many rats, and Rosa ees complain everyday to Gonzales: "Why you not man like Alberto Luis now? See, he have ze beeg house and ze beeg gringo car and ze beeg . . ."

"Ah *querida*," Gonzales ees always reply, "but nobody ees like Alberto; everyone ees hating heem."

"Zey ees Jealous of Alberto, ees why!" Rosa always reply with angriness. "Zey ees jealous of heem because he ees rich. If not zat I ees love you I ees leave you and be Alberto's concubina, even though I too ees hating heem." Zen she always beat her breasts and sigh, "Oh but I ees love you, Gonzales. I ees not know why zis ees, because you ees poor fool fisherman, but *me vuelves loca,* Gonzales, even though you are stupid. I ees love you so much, Gonzales, that if I am not see you one day I ees kill myself!"

And Rosa ees starting to cry then.

And Gonzales, he say nothing, because he know how Alberto Luis have all ze beeg house and Americano gringo Ford car and ze plenty cash, and why Rosa ees loving himself so madly so much.

Ees Gonzales fault, hombre, zat Alberto ees so rich and himself so poor. But he not dare to tell Rosa zis.

If he ees foolish and tell her, she ees sure to knife heem while he ees sleeping. Zen she ees madly sorry and kill herself also.

Ees like zis, hombres:

Gonzales and Alberto zey ees eses from since zey ees bambino, okay? Zey ees always together everywhere.

One day zey go fishing on ze river.

Zey catch zis beeg fish. Ze beeg fish ees gold in color, and zey ees thinking how zey ees sell it to Señor Rosen, ze rich gringo with ze fishtank in ees house.

"Ah, ese," Alberto ees saying, "Today ze Almighty ees smiling on us. If we sell zis gold fish to Señor Rosen, we ees travel to Guadalajara with ze money, and get work zere."

"Ees true, ese," Gonzales ees reply, but ees mind ees not zere. He ees thinking about Rosa, who he ees loving, but who ees not loving heem back. In fact she has tell heem zat she knife heem in ze belly if he ever come near her again, and also that she ees love his friend Alberto Luis not heem.

Gonzales, he has not tell Alberto about zis.

Zen ze fish it ees talk to them from inside ze net. "Ah, señors," it ees say, "you ees not sell me to Señor Rosen, ees you?"

"Ees true, hombre," Gonzales ees reply. "We ees poor hombres— we sell you for money so that we travel to Guadalajara and become rich and señoritas think we too ees sexy."

Alberto too ees nod to zis. "Ees true, hombre. But please not talk when we ees with Señor Rosen until we leave, or he not buy you, si?"

"What if I ees trading my eyes for my freedom?" ze fish ees ask.

"What use ees your eyes?" Gonzales ees asking. "No one ees buy only eyes."

Ze fish ees laughing. "My right eye ees for money. If you ees eat it you ees rich for life, but nobody like you at all—everybody ees hate you. My left eye ees for love; if you ees eat it, you ees have ze señorita you want, and she ees loving you for life like *ella está loca*—like she ees mad—but you ees always poor."

"Are you sure?" zey ask ze fish.

"Ees true," ze fish say. "If ees not true, you come to ze river and catch me again. I not have eyes anymore, how I see you coming?"

But zey still not trust ze fish, so Gonzales ask it, "Are you ze Catholic fish or ze Protestante?"

"Ah, señor, I am ze good Catholic fish; my name ees Frederico."

"In zat case swear by Holy Maria zat you not trick us."

So he swear: "I Frederico ze fish, I ees swear by ze Holy Maria zat I ees tell ze truth."

So zey believe heem.

Ze fish, he ees now remove his eyes and give to zem, and zey ees let heem go back into ze river, and he swim away. Zen zey ees looking at ze two eyes. Ze left one which look like ze heart, and ze right, which look like ze Pesos.

"I ees taking ze love eye," Gonzales ees saying immediately. "You ees taking ze richness. Zen you will be rich, and you ees help me wit ze money when I need, and I ees helping you with ze public relations when ze people ees hating you."

"Why we not divide ze eyes and eat fifty-fifty?" Alberto Luis say. "Zat way we both have ze money and ze love."

"No no," Gonzales say. He ees thinking only zat if he ees share ze love eye with Alberto, Rosa will still be loving Alberto and marrying heem, not himself Gonzales. He ees not wanting zis, so he ees quickly taking and eating ze love eye, before Alberto ees stopping heem.

And Alberto, he ees eating ze richness eye.

Ze fish he ees telling zem the truth. When zey ees come back to town, Rosa ees immediately starting to love Gonzales like ze *mujer loca*, so much zat she ees threatening to knife any woman she see near heem, including his mama, only now Gonzales he ees poor like ze rats in ze Almighty's church.

And Alberto? He ees rich like ze gringo Señor Rosen. However, now everybody ees hating heem like he ees El Diablo himself.

Zat ees my story, yes. It ees strange, me eses, ees it not?

Ring Ring

"Hello . . . ?"

"Hello, Jane. This is Father."

"Fa . . . Father?"

"Surely you recognize my voice, darling."

"But . . . you're dead!"

"Yes, your husband murdered me."

"Mark?"

"Poison."

"But Margaret said your heart . . ."

"I've some bad news for you, dear. Your husband and doctor friend are having an affair."

"Margaret wouldn't; she's my best friend—that's impossible!"

"Surely not as impossible as my phoning you from the afterlife? They killed me so you'd get your inheritance early, and now—"

"Hold on a minute, father, I need to sit down; I feel rather odd."

"I understand, dear. That's what I called about. Mark's just poisoned you too. You've at most fifteen minutes of life remaining."

"No . . . !"

"Afraid so, sweetie. You'll need to hurry now if you want to murder him in retaliation before you die."

Shrink Me

Once there was a man named Mike who had a swimming pool in his head. It was a covered swimming pool—his bald pate flipped over on hinges. Once opened, the upper half of his head was revealed to contain showers and changing rooms for bathers.

Mike's wife Stella swam regularly in his head. He didn't mind this; he only insisted that she use the shower before she did so, to avoid dirtying his mind.

How? Beside his bed Mike kept a bottle labeled 'Shrink Me,' a few drops on the tongue of which reduced Stella to two inches in height.

Mike slept sitting, propped with pillows, so he wouldn't spill.

***

Mike's best friend was a woman named Spike who was a bodybuilder. Spike built all kinds of bodies: male, female, child, and animals even, if an owner wasn't particularly pleased with the way their pet looked.

She had pierced nipples with BIG business adverts hanging from them. The right sign said 'Spike's,' the left 'Bodyshop.'

"You know," Mike told Spike occasionally, "if I wasn't married to *her*, I'd be married to you."

***

For a while now, Mike had been plagued by dirty thoughts. Each time he passed a woman on the street, he'd imagine himself getting 'smudgy' with her. No matter how hard he tried placing the cause, however, he was unable to. In addition, he discovered that every morning his swimming pool was empty.

He became scared that his pool was leaking.

Then one night he discovered that Stella, once she thought him asleep, drank some 'Shrink Me,' and taking bath salts and towel, ran a bubble bath in his head, soaping herself luxuriantly and scrubbing fiercely. Then she pulled the plug (which was a no no) and let the bathwater drain down his throat.

Mike was shocked. He told her so: "I'm shocked that you'd do such a thing."

"I'm sorry, dear; I really am," she replied. "I just want you to know me better—you know we haven't been communicating much of late." She however promised not to take any more bubble baths in his head.

Mike felt okay again for a few days, then suddenly he found himself feeling hungover each morning, in addition to which he felt even dirtier-minded than before.

Suspicion bred investigation, which led to him discovering his wife having a champagne bath in his pool, this time in company of a young man he recognized as a movie producer. After they'd bathed, Stella got up with a thick sheaf of papers in hand, and began declaiming loudly, "I, puny mortal, am the goddess of this waterspout; who art thou that disturbest my pools?" and other such like.

"I was auditioning," she said sweetly when Mike confronted her. "It's only till I get the part."

After this an uneasy calm prevailed. Stella didn't get the part, and the producer never called again.

***

Then one day, the bottle of 'Shrink Me' ran out. Stella packed up and left Mike, saying she couldn't live with a man she couldn't get into.

"I'll buy you another," he wept, but she was already gone.

***

After his wife's desertion, Mike began literally falling apart. He'd wake each morning to find bits of himself lying on the bed. After checking to ensure that he hadn't spilt any water during the night, he'd pick up either eye or nose and stick it back on his face.

***

He told Spike his problem. "You're a bodybuilder," he said, "I need renovation—I'm breaking up."

"I suspect your clutch is broken," Spike said. She unbricked Mike's chest to investigate. "I was right," she said. "It *is* your clutch—it's eroded through."

"My clutch?" Mike asked in incomprehension.

"What holds you together." She held a mirror before his open chest, pulling flesh-bricks wide apart, so he could look into it. He saw that attached to his skeleton were a mass of metal hands holding his organs in place. One hand gripped his stomach, another his liver; and so on. Peering up and down inside himself, he made out yet other hands holding his arm and leg joints in place.

Spike pointed to the hand holding his heart. Its wrist was rusted almost clean through. In addition, two fingers had fallen off. "*That's* your clutch," she said. "You need a replacement. I've got a spare, but . . ."

The 'but' was that Mike would have to give up his swimming pool. "Do I really have to?" he asked disconsolately.

"You can see yourself what the problem is: your clutch was damaged—rusted—by your ex-wife draining the water from your swimming pool down here each time she took a bath. Actually, it was the bath soap that did it." She looked hard at Mike. "Look, if you don't let go of your waterhead, you could eventually die of heartbreakdown."

Without real choice in the matter, Mike agreed. He let Spike both fix his clutch and remove his swimming pool.

***

Occasionally, after Spike had renovated him, Mike would awaken at night to stampeding sounds inside his head. Spike had however super-glued his skull shut (as well as padlocking it), so he couldn't flip its top back to have a look.

"It's okay," she'd tell him laughing. "Nothing to worry about. Remember what they say about empty vessels and noise."

This comment hurt Mike greatly but he'd say nothing.

***

Mike and Spike fell in love, got married, and had a son called Bike, so named because he had two handlebars growing out of his temples, as well as headlights for eyes.

After Bike's birth, Spike told Mike the truth: "My nipple piercings won't let me breastfeed, darling, so while renovating you, I built a dairy farm inside your head."

"Oh no, you didn't!" Mike said, horrified.

Just hold on a minute, honey dearest," Spike said, getting out a bottle of 'Shrink Me' from her bag. After dropping a few drops on her tongue, she opened Mike's left ear like a door and climbed inside him to milk the cows, so she could give Bike his breakfast.

Good Medicine

Brad hated women.

It wasn't his fault, but his parents'.

His mother was a loud brassy woman with a chainsaw tongue; his father a weak, insecure man whom his wife's never-ending insults had made seek solace in alcohol. Brad's father's drinking, however, had made him violent, and after a while, when his wife insulted him, he beat her up, often bloodily.

And yet the couple had remained married.

Brad had silently absorbed all this. While he disliked his father for being a weakling, he *hated* his mother, particularly since she'd tongue-lashed him into insecurity too.

He'd run away from home at sixteen; drifting and taking on a succession of jobs.

Finally he'd had his first girlfriend, the emotional programming of his early years making him select Tyla, a woman as loud and irritating as his mother had been, with the inevitable results—unable to stomach her tongue, he'd snapped under the influence of drink and beaten her to within six inches of death.

He'd done five years in the state pen for aggravated assault—a reduced sentence because the judge's son was an old classmate of his.

Once he left jail, Brad had decided it was safer to hate women than to love them.

He'd found no reasons to change his mind since then, and had had no relationships. It had occurred to him to simply date men instead, but here he had major reservations. Men were great for companionship and conversation, but romance . . . ?

Then the alien came.

***

66

Trina hated men. Here there was no ambiguous sublimations as in Brad's case. She hated men because they'd abused her. She hated her father for not loving her, and her four elder brothers for beating her up regularly. Her mother had died when she was four so she'd had no protection from them.

Most of all she hated the drunk male driver who'd left her permanently in a wheelchair with a broken spine, and she hated all the men who never looked at her, only at her glossy friends.

"Homosexuality stalks in dark recesses of my mind," she was fond of telling Trish, her glossiest friend. "In daytime visions alternate sexuality calls sweetly unto me. I currently seek the last male straw which breaks my heterosexual camel's back."

No lesbians came into her daytime actuality, however. So Trina contented herself with hating men with all the passion she would have used to love them.

Then the alien came.

**

The alien was actually a robot, a silvery manlike humandroid with telescoping eyes. It arrived late one afternoon in a battered spaceship it parked out in the Arizona Desert, and set up shop in a prefabricated kiosk: 'Dr. Sigmund Droid, Psychiatric Cures—Phobia Specialist.'

First there was skepticism in the nearby towns about the new 'Doctor,' then a few people went into the desert and were cured of their fears of snakes and rats, then there was a deluge of patients and Brad and Trina went too.

**

"I had a woman in here yesterday with a similar problem to yours," Dr. Sigmund Droid told Brad after hearing him out. "Only in her case she hated *men*."

"Why would she do that?" Brad asked, "Men are so cool. *Women* are the problem."

"I'm sure Ms. Trina will think the same when I tell her your views of *her* sex," the robot psychiatrist replied. "That, however, is neither here nor there—it helps neither of you. I however have a solution in mind—one which might cure you both. Are you willing to try it?"

Brad nodded. A few hours later, Trina nodded too.

Brad and Trina met in Dr. Sigmund Droid's office and hated each another appropriately for an appropriate amount of time. Then the doctor placed metal caps (wired to a humming gizmo on its desk) over their heads and flicked a few switches.

The gizmo hummed louder and louder, then stopped. Dr. Sigmund Droid removed the caps from both their heads and stepped back.

"There, both of you should be cured now."

"I don't feel any different," Brad said.

"Me neither," Trina said.

"Oh, but you do," Dr. Droid said, "Try hating each other now."

They tried, they really did.

Brad found that rather than hate the pretty woman stuck in the wheelchair, he now hated his dad who'd neglected him as a child, his four brothers who'd beaten the crap out of him, and he hated worst of all the driver who'd put him permanently in a wheelchair . . . Shocked, he stopped hating for a moment and examined himself to ensure he was still whole. No, he didn't hate women any more.

He however HATED those DISGUSTING MEN with a passion.

Trina made the same discovery. She now HATED WOMEN. Most of all she hated her foul-mouthed mother who'd made an alcoholic out of her loving father, and made her beat up her first girlfriend (who wasn't any better than her stupid mother—YES she HAD been a lesbian that ONE time, SO WHAT!?) into a bloody pulp, and go to jail for it . . . Men were OKAY. But women? Shit, they were worse than crap. She HATED them.

Dr. Sigmund Droid smiled at the pair.

"Like I said, you're both fine now—perfectly ready to cope with romance."

***

"This is some weird shit, Trina," Brad said, "But I think you look cute in that wheelchair. You wanna go get a drink?"

"Yeah, let's."

"Okay, but don't get worried if I beat up a few guys. You know, I just can't stand the sight of those disgusting pigs ogling my girl."

"Me, it's those waitresses I can't stand, all slinky like snakes, trying to snare my boyfriend."

"Boyfriend, eh?"

Now properly maladjusted, they lived together happily ever after.

Liquid Husband

I goes up. Room. Apple gun awaits me. I will fruit-kill my brains out all over the wall for Maria.

Maria loves not I. I've no money. I'm the governor of the state of poverty. Virtual-reality economics has leeched me of alpha-maleness. I'm Goth cabaret.

Suicide is a pathetic realization.

Die I, loves Maria other men voraciously. Insatiable fuckness on my grave. Boning over bones.

Die Maria, happiness grows in I like graveyard lilies.

Kill I Maria. Kill I later. Maybe.

***

I goes down.

My gun needs violentation. Bloodletting validation, meaning for its rustproof orchard-grown unlife.

As I go, I load my apple gun with apple bullets. Maria is the apple of my eye. It's poetically appropriate I apple her ass.

Hail Maria! White widow in black leotards. Eight arm-legs woman, Mexican-Hindu goddess.

Maria spider dangles stickywebs in church bell tower. Eats previous liquid husband—man flows dead like unbottled Zinfandel.

Erotic teeth flash between her legs. Sexy death. Maria's sexiness vacuums me up irresistibly.

Mans is the moth, groin-cat teeth our candle.

But despite all its protestations to the contrary, pussy needs mouse, or it will die of hunger.

I church mouse to the belfry door.

Knock knock!!!

"Who's there?"

"I."

"I who?"

I enters.

The bone-colored widow in black flows around me like crypt-rotted silk. An non-holy virgin lookalike. Segmented eyes of a love-starved lioness. Octet legarms gesticulate non-reasonably.

Maria speaks. "Dios capture my abusive husband."

The ground and walls grow stone hands. These cement-plaster limbs disarm me. They hold me up between them, a sacrifice lacking an alter ego.

In midair I dangle, erotic barbequed man roasting in lust.

"I'll kill you for love!" I shriek at Maria.

"I'll kill your love for me," Maria coldly replies.

We nod in agreement. Death is death, an irreversible sharing of violence. It matters not who kills who.

But Maria's sexy is EVIL.

Stone hands feed me my apple gun. Orchard-metal fractures my teeth, fills my mouth with indigestible longing for her. Painful swallows fly down my throat to corrosive nests in my belly.

My enzymes digest the metal truth of citrus green. Gun-apples aren't my favorite food.

My belly button barrel bulges bellward. Intestinal trigger happy coils.

Apple bullets fire out of my navel, ringing out church bells.

Below, the lady priest calls for the worship of black-widowhood.

She announces the new husband rules: "Love vagina or die trying."

Hailing Marias makes my tragedy worthwhile.

I kill not Iself no more for love. Maria kills me much better without even trying.

I goes inside her—lamb is to slaughters.

The East Side of the House

"Sun dies in the West, but rise in the East,
So stay in the west to avoid the beast."

– New Japanese Proverb

"It's HUGE," Macy said.

Jim affected a nod. Looking at their new home, all he could remember were the old salesman's words: "It's a great house, but with one catch—*Never, ever*, go to the east side of the grounds in the afternoon. Morning, evening, even night's fine, but not afternoon."

Weird advice, but which seemed to have been adhered to by the previous residents. The east side of the compound was a jungle. Jim doubted it had started out that way, but now . . . The grass and bushes grew in such profusion that it looked like part of the Amazon. All it lacked was a river and some anaconda. looking at it, however, Jim was uncertain it lacked anaconda.

"Ugh, we'll need to clear the bushes," Macy said.

***

The oddest thing about the house were the animal statues. All were of wild animals—jungle beasts, carnivores. The statues were in two rows, arranged between the house and its 'forest' on high pedestals, the plinths staggered so no statue blocked another from view. Macy observed this the second day after they'd moved in while staring down from their bedroom window. She called Jim's attention to it.

"It's creepy," she said with a shiver, pointing.

He looked, saw what she meant. The afternoon sun's rays had thrown the animal shadows on the 'jungle,' arranging them in a line like they were walking across the top of the grass. In addition, the sun's warming the air was making the shadows wax and wane as though they were alive.

"We *need* to clear the bushes," Macy said.

Jim nodded.

***

Jim began clearing the bush on the house's east side two days later. Macy was insistent it had to go, and Jim had discovered he'd no alternative but to tackle the task himself.

To his surprise, all six gardening companies he'd called had declined the job once he gave them his address, two without even bothering to wait and hear what he wanted. Finally he called Mr Macking, the house agent.

"It's what I was trying to explain when I sold it to you," Mr Macking said. "There's an old superstition about the place—its bad luck."

"But that's silly!"

"Maybe so, but still, no-one's dared clear the bushes since . . ." Macking's voice lapsed into silence.

"Since what?"

"Okay, it's more than superstition. The last owner was found half-eaten on the edge of the uncleared patch . . ."

"What!?"

"It was about three in the afternoon when neighbors heard the shrieking. He'd ignored the instructions not to go there in the afternoon, see?"

Jim was stumped. "I don't get it. The police . . . ?"

"Won't go near there."

"The zoo then."

"Them neither."

"Let me try to get this straight: There's a wild animal living in the grounds of this building, which for some reason no one's willing to track and kill, and you sold it to me. You didn't even fence it off. I'm going to sue—"

"You'll lose the case," the estate agent interrupted him, his tone indicating his patience was wearing thin. "Listen, Mr. Baker, there's absolutely no danger to you or anyone else in the house . . ."

"I consider a wild animal—"

Macking's voice was cold. ". . . As long as you don't go into that patch in the afternoon. Have a nice day, Mr. Baker."

Jim found himself listening to the dial tone.

He narrated the conversation to Macy. "We're moving," he said finally. "Just as soon as—"

"I like this place," she interrupted him sweetly. "Can't you clear away the weeds yourself?"

"That," Jim said, pointing out-window at the offensive patch of vegetation, the hot afternoon sun once again etching the statue shadows on its surface, *"Is a jungle.* How? . . . Where do you expect me to begin?"

Macy pointed. "At *that* edge. If you're *scared*, work in the mornings."

Jim felt like he'd been stabbed.

"Scared?"

Macy smiled a saccharine smile, knowing she had him. "Well, it is creepy, dearest. The shadows, the superstitions . . ."

"Okay, I'll do it."

***

Saturday morning, Jim began work with a pair of machetes and a lawn mower. The grass reached well over his head, and to his surprise, he discovered that once inside the bushy patch, he was unable to see the animal statues lining it at all.

It was a cool day. He worked till eleven in the morning, forced to stop when he came on a patch of bamboo which had no business being there. He examined it cautiously, almost expecting to see monkeys chattering atop the longer stems.

He sat down, back against a bamboo stem, to rest. He'd so far cleared a hundred meter square patch, about an eighth of the offending vegetation. Working at his current rate he'd be done in five days.

Macy brought Jim a glass of lemonade, went back into the house. He drank it down, made himself comfortable, dozed off.

***

He was wakened by a growl. He opened his eyes, scanned the sky. The sun was well past its zenith. It had to be close to two o'clock. Damn, he'd slept into the forbidden afternoon hours.

Then he noticed the oddity.

There was a shadow facing him. He blinked, wiped his eyes with the back of his hand. It *was* a shadow, that of a lion. The only problem was that it was standing upright, *out of* the ground.

As he watched in horror, it thickened.

As Jim stared back at the animal statues by the house, now understanding the reason for the warning he'd been given, other wild-animal-shadows walked out of the bush to join the lion.

'Thickening' as they came, they advanced on Jim, with hunger in their eyes and bared shadow teeth . . .

.

In Reverso . . .

One day, Chris saw black and white people fighting.

"Why are they fighting?" he asked.

"Because though they are the same they look different," was the answer he received.

Chris pondered a way to remedy this till one occurred to him.

Later that night when they were sleeping, he bleached all the black people white and painted all the white people black. Satisfied with the solution he went to sleep, saying, "This will help them to see that they are one and the same."

But in the morning when they awoke, the black and white people only saw that they were still different in color from each other and at once resumed fighting.

Entertaining Spider

"I've never eaten a transsexual before," Spider told Jenny Loveless. While speaking, it scrutinized her minutely.

"I assure you we taste just the same as everyone else does," Jenny replied it, frantically trying to figure a way out of this latest mess her greed had gotten her into.

She was currently suspended ten feet in the air, wrapped in stinging coils of toilet-fetid web. Her gun lay twenty feet away.

Spider stopped studying Jenny. It walked over to Millicent's broken corpse. It ripped off her left leg and began eating it. Jenny shut her eyes, wished she could plug her ears to the sound of breaking bone, shredding flesh . . .

***

Jenny Loveless was still unsure what had gone wrong. She and Millicent Ball had broken into Apartment 29, only it hadn't been there, just a ruined space full of broken furniture and . . . Spider.

"Look out!" she'd yelled, turning to flee. Next thing, she'd heard the dull thuds of Spider's fangs piercing Millie's body, then felt burning web lasso her own.

***

"You look delicious," Spider told her, "packed with juice. I can't wait to suck you dry."

An idea occurred to Jenny; one so absurd it seemed worth a try. "Let me tell you a story," she said.

"Uh?" Spider stroked her face with a hairy foreleg. Jenny felt as if several cockroaches were walking on her. "What?"

"Entertainment while you're eating Millicent—so you don't get bored. Storytelling's my profession. I promise you this one'll be good."

"Oh, I don't know," Spider said. "It seems creepy to get on too familiar terms with your meals."

With nerves of steel, Jenny concealed her desperation. "Look, humor me. Okay, so you're going to eat me afterwards. Still, it's considered sporting to grant a condemned man's last request."

"You're not a *man*."

"Woman, then."

"You're not *that* either." Spider was genuinely bemused by her androgyny.

Her fear gave way to exasperation. "WHAT HAS MY GENDER GOT TO DO WITH ANYTHING? JUST LET ME TELL YOU A FUCKING STORY!" Her voice calmed a little. "Back off, sit down, eat Millie's right leg or ass, and *listen*. Entertainment is good for digestion."

"Oh, alright," Spider said, taken aback by her vehemence, confused by her insistence on this oddness. The leg it'd already eaten had also put it in a more amenable mood than it had been in when the pair had broken into its lair.

After following Jenny's suggestion and ripping off Millicent's right leg, it sat and listened.

"Once upon a time there was a beautiful, *beautiful* woman named Scheherazade Clinton," Jenny began. "This happened a long time ago, when time was still reckoned in A.D. and B.C. and not A.G. like we do now, loooooooong before Gutuz the Barrier locked everyone down here.

"Now, beautiful Scheherazade was in love with a young hunchback named Aladdin, only he didn't like her in return, being more interested in a female genius . . ."

***

Spider was surprised at how much it liked the story. True, it was *very* long, but it was great to hear about the evil king Osama, and about the good king Obama who'd fought against him, both of them really wanting Aladdin's lamp and genius girlfriend, and also about the Doll-Fins who'd tried to mediate but had been turned into fish burgers for their troubles by Osama and sold to Japanese corporations, and also how Scheherazade Clinton, seeing that Aladdin disliked her, gave some magic beans to Jack and told him to climb the beanstalk and get the Three Blind Mice Musketeers, and then . . ."

Listening in keen multi-eyed interest, Spider ate the rest of Millicent's limbs and her head also. They tasted *gooooooood*— entertainment really did help digestion.

Jenny Loveless coldly watched Millicent's corpse disappear. She spun the story on endlessly, talking for hours, knowing she was talking to keep herself alive.

She spoke and spoke and spoke until the sky lightened.

***

"Oops, it's morning," Spider said. "I never eat after 6 a.m.—gives me really bad gas through the day. Tell you what—I'll eat you tonight, after you finish the tale of Scheherazade and the magic lamp with the genius, of course."

"Of *course*," Jenny said, smiling sweetly. "You don't mind, do you?"

"No, not at all." To Jenny's horror, it was currently in the process of transforming itself into a twenty-something-year-old man. As it altered, so did their surroundings, till finally they were in a normal bedsitter, with Jenny tied to the bed. Where Millicent's corpse had been, now stood a large freezer. Jenny had no doubts what it contained.

Transformation complete, Spider went into the bathroom to brush his teeth. He came out again fully dressed in a suit complete with tie.

Spider, now the quintessential human, picked up his briefcase and walked over to Jenny. His name tag read: 'Spyder Mann— Communications Supervisor.'

He smiled, said, "Time I was getting to work. I'll see you tonight."

"Oh, I've just remembered another interesting old tale," Jenny said, gazing coldly into Spider's ice-blue eyes. "You'll *love* this one. It's the tale of the War between the Undead Statues of Liberty and the Lost Kings of Hollywood. The hero's a potter named Harrison who rides a Trojan horse."

With relief she read the interest in Spider's eyes.

"Is it a *loooooong* tale?" Spider asked. "I really *must* eat you soon."

She smiled sweetly. "I shouldn't take too long, but just in case, buy some burgers for both of us—that way we won't starve before you're ready to eat me."

"No need to buy food," Spider said nicely, "I've still got your friend's torso in the freezer. I don't mind sharing that with you."

The door shut behind him. Bound neck, wrist and ankle to the bed, Jenny Loveless resumed her frantic search for a means of escape, before she ran out of stories to tell Spider.

Number One

This isn't Speed Racer, or some other animation from the old days.

This is reality TV at its best (or worst); blood and guts smeared on tarmac like spilt ketchup, explosions at high speed cooking flesh and plastic crisps. All captured in Ultra High Definition.

The mortal fast food joint of the pseudo-evolved savage.

The triumph of the lack of corporate ethics delivered in glossy color to a public in love with us, the ultimate expression of its decadence.

The subsonic screams of jetcars pushed to their limits, metal and rubber shrilling in pain, are unknown to any but we racers, we who the public dote upon.

My name, in case you're blind and deaf, is John Speed.

I'm Number One. The jetcar race king.

***

In our races there are no rules except one—whoever wins, wins. The only restriction on vehicle design is that it be wingless, have wheels, and a jet engine.

Ride the jetcar grid, *survive*, win—in that order.

Jetcar racing is as close to legally sanctioned murder (and suicide—if you lose concentration) as it gets.

***

For the first time in five years I lost. It was a narrow thing, a split second of indecision: fear of collision with the car ahead.

I shrug it off—put it down to exhaustion.

It happens again. I suddenly find myself making mistakes I've never done before.

***

I see my shrink, Sigmund Droid. Sig's a mandroid—a human shaped AI-controlled mechanism with delusions of grandeur. He thinks he's smarter than a man, seems to constantly forget that he runs on a program *we* developed.

"Sexual jealousy," he says after hearing me out, "the primary failing of the evolved ape. You're married of course?"

Rhetorical question. Everyone on the planet knows my new wife, the beautiful Selena Chow, so physically perfect no one notices she's perfectly stupid. I *love* her being an airhead—It's great not to have to spend time better used perfecting my skills emotionally fencing with someone trying to validate her status as my equal.

"From your explanation, I can track your current crisis down to one source . . ." Sigmund begins.

I wait.

". . . You're scared of dying and losing your wife," he ends.

He's right.

"But what can I do?" I whimper, desperately grasping for hope I doubt exists. For myself at least, it seems the end has truly come.

"Become a machine," Sigmund says laconically.

"I'm human. Flesh and blood. I thought you'd have noticed that since I've been coming here."

"Mere terminology. Metal or flesh-and-blood, a machine is a machine. To us droids, you humans are simply imperfect mechanisms with emotional problems. If you wish to remain *Number One*, evolution is clearly the next step."

"Fuck you, Sig," I grumble. But revealingly, I don't stamp out in anger. Rather, I lean forward. "How do you propose I go about becoming a machine?"

Sigmund explains in more detail than I care to know. When he's done spouting, I curse him loudly, *then* stamp off in disgust.

***

Descending in the elevator, my mind boils with what he's told me. Essentially, I must become a eunuch—not just in terms of losing my genitals, but also in terms of having my brain surgically altered so I no longer even feel any desire for sexual gratification. Or for Selena.

Impossible of course. The pleasures of the flesh are beautiful . . . Selena Chow is even *more* beautiful; it will be impossible to see her in the arms of another man, imagine her in his embrace, in his bed . . . his doing to her all the things I'll no longer be able to do. I'd kill her first.

It is clear I need to change psychiatrists. Maybe I'll try a flesh-and-blood one again.

***

Losing my next two races gives me a new perspective. Already I sense those who worship me whispering that my day is over, that it's time to change religious allegiance.

***

Before making love one night, Selena suggests that I commit suicide, crash my car during a race. Go out in a blaze of glory while I'm *still* Number One. And of course leave her all my money.

I laugh in appreciation of her stupidity. She's fantastic. Of what use is a smart wife when you don't need one—when all her brains are are catalysts, igniting in her the continual need to prove to you that she truly is your intellectual equal? With lovely Selena I lack that problem. Her essential self is her external package. What you see is *all* you get.

Few men understand the freedom such a woman brings with her.

***

Later, sated from her flesh, I consider her words more seriously.

Unpleasantly, they ring with truth. I could not endure the fall from being jetcar's Number One. It is either I do as she suggests, or as Sigmund Droid suggests.

***

I go to see Sigmund Droid again. He's *very* correct about my problem being sexual jealousy.

Since marrying Selena I have killed three men. None of my victims were jetcar competitors, or anyone important: their only claims on my attentions were the 'desiring' way they looked at my wife.

I dispatched all three fools messily, but carefully. Murder is easy if you're motivated enough.

***

I lose one more race. About to perform the daredevil maneuver that would *assure* my victory, thoughts of my death and Selena's subsequent remarriage paralyze me.

My slumping performance is now Earth's hottest news topic.

***

I make my decision.

Tomorrow, I *will* go under the surgeon's knife. To begin my evolution. To become *perfect*. Free from error-inducing emotional and sexual strain.

To be truly Number One.

As for my beloved vapid wife Selena Chow, if I can't enjoy her amorous embraces, no one will. She too will go under the knife, only she won't be waking up afterwards.

Then the races! Bring it on, you testosterone-burdened primitives!

Señor Ogre
(A Legend of Bizarro Mexico)

Ah now, my son, you listen to zis tale. Ees about ze great Carlos Riviera, and how he save his lover Angelina from ze Ogre who live under ze lake.

You see, back in ze day, Señor Ogre, he ees take many many beautiful señoritas away from zis town. Even your mother, my son, Señor Ogre he ees take her away; ees why your older brother Pauli have three eyes and four legs now, but zat is not zees story—I tell you zat one another time.

Now Señor Ogre, he ees beeg, and he live under ze lake.

I hear many stories about Señor Ogre, one ees zat he ees a gringo, an Americano soldier zat escape from ze Americano militante hospital somewhere; another story ees zat Señor Ogre he ees fighing ze Iraqs and zey gass him with ze bad chemicals.

I not know which story ees correct, but I know he ees very ugly. He ees red-skinned, and has a big mouth with teeth like ze alligators Luiz Sanchez always catch. Also he have four legs like your older brother Pauli do, and bullets not kill heem.

I know zis ees true about ze bullets, because when I go with your uncle Diego to try rescue your mama, Señor Ogre he eat our guns when we shoot him. He also eat ze truck we drive, and as Diego he ees driving, he also eat Diego. Ees why your aunty Juana ees ze loco now—ze crazy. Ah, my son—Juana, she really love Diego; may God and ze Holy Maria rest ees departed soul.

But I tell zis story another time too.

Soon Señor Ogre take all ze pretty señoritas—ze mamacitas—in ze town; only ze ugly señoritas remain for us hombres to marry. We not complain—ees God who make ugly señoritas too; so we marry them, though some men run away to marry pretty mamacitas from other towns.

But now Señor Ogre he go too far. He begin to kidnap ze ugly señoritas too.

Papa Riviera, Carlos' father, confront Señor Ogre about zis, as Ogre ees about returning to ees house beneath ze lake with Angelina in ees sack on ees back.

"You not take my son Carlos's señorita away, Señor Ogre," he say, waving his walking stick like it ze Mexican flagpole. "What only you do with so many senoritas? Ees Americano selfishness!"

Señor Ogre push heem out of ze way.

But Papa Riviera ees not wise and cowardly like we who run and hide, see? No he is very brave and very foolish. He hit Señor Ogre on ze head with ze stick.

Señor Ogre ees angry. He turn and bite Papa Riviera. He not bite all of him, no! He is only eat one bite of him from top to down. But that bite kill heem! Yes! He eat his head and all his chest and stomach with that one bite, but his arms and legs still remain. So Papa Riviera now look like a 'U' with arms and legs.

But he ees dead. Si, ees dead.

You look surprised? Ow ees zees possible? I not tell you zat Señor Ogre is very big? No? Ah, I forget, my son—he ees very big. Almost like your schoolbus. His head too, ees big like Pauli your brother.

But don't fear, my son.

You see, after Señor Ogre kill Papa Riviera and steal Angelina, Carlos come back home from ze city. And he ees mad zat his papa ees dead.

Ah yes, Carlos, he ees mad.

He call all of us cowards, and we say ees true we are cowards, but how can we fight Ogre?

So Carlos go and meet Black Magic Lucia. Lucia, she is a witch, very powerful, very bad, very old. Carlos promise to marry her if she defeat Señor Ogre for heem.

Why he need to promise zis? Because Black Magic Lucia ees so ugly no man ever propose to her in her life—ees ze reason why she become a witch.

But all Carlos is want revenge. Ees not thinking deeply about anything elze at ze time.

Black Magic Lucia ees happy to be getting married, so she help Carlos.

She give heem a wrapped package, and tell him ees not to open it as ees full of ze magic to defeat Señor Ogre, but ees to dive into ze river with it and swim down to Señor Ogre's house. When he get zere he ees to give Ogre zis package *before* he ees fighting heem.

Carlos do as she say. He dive into ze lake. He dive deep, and find zat Ogre live inside a fish. Ees beeg fish, almost as beeg as Mexico City.

Ze fish is called Augustine. Ees true—he has nametag. Ees name is Augustine and he works at ze post office.

Augustine allow Señor Ogre to live inside heem becos, ze señoritas Ogre is kidnapping is helping clean Augustine's belly. Ze fish Augustine has many windows in his belly.

Ees what all our beautiful mamacitas spend all zere time doing, washing and polishing Augustine's windows. Ees sad, no?

So Carlos swim down to Augustine, and knock on one of Augustine's eyes which ees also a door.

Carlos tell us zat he ees shaking with fear when Señor Ogre open ze eye door, but he ees brave and give him ze package like Black Magic Lucia tell him to.

Señor Ogre take ze package from Carlos Riviera. He open it and pull out a little booklet from inside it. Carlos say now Ogre, he ees suddenly very surprised, like he ees not believe what he sees. He open ze booklet, and read it. When next he look at Carlos Riviera, he ees smiling ees beeg alligator smile.

"Thanks, dude," ees what he say. Only zat: 'Thanks, dude.' And he turn immediately and enter his bedroom and begin to pack all his ownings into ees suitcase, while Carlos Riviera ees wanting to fight.

But Ogre, ees not fighting Carlos at all.

Ah, my son, you wonder what ees going on?

Ees like zis: You see Black Magic Lucia has long ago stolen Señor Ogre's passport. He does not know that she take eet. With no passport he cannot leave Mexico. He want to go to Paris, but he ees stuck here as illegal immigrant.

He ees *hiding* from ze authorities under ze river inside Augustine. Now Carlos Riviera return hees passport to heem. Now he ees free to go away from Mexico, and he go.

He apologize to Carlos Riviera for biting his papa, then he help him return all our kidnapped señoritas to ze town again, so Carlos ees become ze beeg hero. Then Señor Ogre, he ride ze next truck for Veracruz, and board ze ship zere—you know he ees too beeg for ze airplane.

I hear he ees ze BEEG movie producer in France now—Tony Ogrini.

Everyone thank Holy Maria zat ze Ogre he ees gone.

So everything ees good now, no? Si, except for Carlos Riviera, who get rid of Señor Ogre for us.

Why? Because though Carlos Riviera frees all ze beautiful girls and even Angelina, who he love even though she not beautiful, ze problem now ees Carlos cannot marry any of zem, because he has promise to marry Black Magic Lucia, who ees old and ugly like Satan.

Carlos ees very angry, but he can do nothing. If he not marry Black Magic Lucia, she magic him into ze frog. So he marry Lucia, and though he is not happy, we all give him money so he ees become very rich now.

Die, You Fluffy Sonofabitch!

Leslie Ryder couldn't sleep. Her pillow seemed to keep squirming beneath her head, wobbling like a set of breasts.

The comparison depressed her; she'd just had a fight with her girlfriend Monica, who had great breasts.

Leslie winced with displeasure. *Monica always overreacts to trivia.* At the moment, she was uncertain what they'd been arguing over. Their fight had begun somewhere definite (she imagined), and next moment, without warning had segued into something else, quite unrelated. Then their mild spat had freefallen into a general airing of grievances that hadn't existed five minutes ago.

Finally Monica had screamed at Leslie. "Listen, you selfish dyke— I never want to see you again!"

Leslie hadn't been able to resist asking, "Does that include booty calls?"

Monica had glared back, slammed the door and stalked off home.

No rush, Leslie had decided, *I'll let her cool off overnight, call her up tomorrow; once I eat her pussy, she'll forgive me.*

But now, this damn pillow had reminded her of their fight, of Monica's lovely angry face, of her even more lovely body (oh, what a delicious big ass and breasts Monica had), which had warmed her on so, so many nights.

Oh, just the memory of Monica's hot bod had Leslie all het up, raring to go down on her, to spread those plump Arizona-bred thighs and bury her tongue deep in the revealed meaty vagina, sucking the female juices out.

Only Monica and her sweet pussy had already gone.

She argued with herself. *Shit! You should have thought of that before pissing her off. It wasn't my fault. So? It doesn't matter whose fault it was— saying 'sorry' keeps couples together. You disagree? Okay, who's fucking alone now when they'd rather be fucking?*

Her pillow seemed to shake again. Frustrated as a fly locked out of a cesspool, Leslie Ryder sat up in bed and turned on the bedside light.

On an sudden eerie feeling that something was wrong, she turned and stared at her pillow.

Her pillow was wobbling. She first gaped at it, then leapt out of bed when it began swelling like it was being inflated.

While a feeling of dread filled her breasts like implants, Leslie watched her pillow get bigger, its quilted patchwork surface covering over with pink quills.

She mused a moment. The pink quills made the swollen pillow look rather cute.

(Outside, the night hung black. Beneath it, Boston, MA. was shadows and squares of light. Somewhere in that city was Monica, beautiful and gorgeous but angry Monica.)

Then a seam ripped open along the pillow's length and fluffy stuffing spilled out of it. Leslie instantly noted the long uneven pin-like teeth inside the pillow. Above the new mouth blinked two pink eyes. Evil eyes that watched her.

Not taking her gaze of it, Leslie edged sideways to the dresser by the window, by which was propped an old sword.

The pillow tracked her motion, it turned its mouth towards her, bared its iron teeth with clear evil intent.

It hissed at Leslie.

Fuck this! she thought and grabbed the heavy sword by its bone hilt. Weapon raised overhead, she leapt at the pillow. It reared upright, tried to bite her, but she ducked its squirming movements.

She maneuvered around it and stabbed it behind its mouth, forcing the sword down deep and true into its fluffy substance. The pillow's mouth slammed shut. She kept it clamped down like a pinned insect.

It began whimpering. Leslie had the sense that it was pleading for mercy.

She granted no such favors. In these bizarre times, in this bizarre city, with Hell just floors beneath her feet, to be weak was to shortly be dead.

"Fuck you!" she yelled. With all her strength, she forced the blade down through the pillow's substance. It was hard work—there seemed to be bones inside the thing now. Bright blood spurted from the pillow, gushed and gushed red, poured like from a shattered water pipe. Desperate not to die, the pillow flailed and fought.

"Die, you fluffy sonofabitch!"

Then it was over: the pillow went limp beneath Leslie. She relaxed, relieved that it was dead.

She backed away from it, stood regarding it.

The dead pillow now seemed burst open—a red fruit someone had squeezed a trifle too hard. In addition, her bed was as sodden with blood as if she'd just mass-murdered a concentration camp of people atop it. *Okay, that's an exaggeration, but still . . . What the . . . ?*

Leslie Ryder wondered why her pillow had suddenly become sentient and started this crap. And she was definitely glad Monica had left for home before it did. Monica had absolutely no spine—the little pussy would have been shrieking the building down now.

Leslie sat opposite the bed and glared at her dead pillow. Slowly, her adrenalin rush subsided. Her battle-rage was replaced with disappointment that the weird conflict was over.

Then followed depression—her mind replaying the night's previous event: her quarrel with Monica.

Seeing Monica's beautiful face in her mind, Leslie was struck by a sudden horny weakness that made her legs tremble.

This was just what she didn't need at the moment. No girlfriend in her bed, and to aggravate her loneliness, no damn pillow to squeeze in her place.

She thought awhile then picked up her phone. *Might as well eat humble pie, call Monica and make up, go sleep over at her house—at least her pillows didn't squirm.*

Leslie Ryder reconsidered. *Or maybe I just never noticed them doing so—I always sleep with my head cradled on her soft breasts.*

Soft Silky Skin

Oh, what lovely skin!

Ruby ran her fingers through the hairs of his chest, pinching his nipples hard.

Her nipples hardened in sympathy. Her breasts felt electrified.

Giggling, she let her fingers delve deeper into his crotch and play in his blonde pubic bush. She reached lower, gripped his soft cock, played with his balls.

She placed her nose to his back and smelt it. His male musk tingled in her nostrils. The scent coming off him made her clitoris tingle with erotic anticipation. Her pussy dripped juice like a squeezed orange.

Ruby thought her arousal down. They'd make love later, for sure, but still . . . His skin . . . so smooth.

She licked his neck like a dog, feeling the short hairs at the nape tickle her tongue. His long blonde locks mingled with hers.

Oh, he was so lovely, Ruby almost couldn't wait.

But not now, not yet . . .

She hung the murdered hitch-hiker's soft silky skin up on her washing line and re-entered the cabin with an axe to chop up the rest of him.

Venice

Jenny Loveless saw the scythe whirling through the air towards her at the last reaction-possible moment. She ducked backwards; it slashed the portion of air her neck had occupied and vanished.

She'd however ducked too far back. She lost her balance and pitched back over the quay-side into the black water beneath.

She fell flat, floating downward under the spell of gravity.

The water beckoned her; her reflection rose from its depths, rushed to welcome her falling self to their collision.

When she was six feet above the water, its surface suddenly altered, its glass smoothness bursting upward at points, forming shimmering liquid knives perpendicular to its surface.

Jenny Loveless screamed as she was impaled on water. She hung in space, transfixed on water spikes, spurting blood.

I'm dying, she thought.

She *was* dying. Her blood—her life—streamed from her multitude of punctures. The water welcomed her crimson flow into itself, momentarily dissolving it into darkness.

Jenny Loveless felt her mind darken.

A scene in a nightmare, her body floated over black water; her blood traced rivulets down the water spears.

A mustached gondolier clambered aboard her, poled her water-suspended form back into the canals of Venice.

***

She awoke in a bright cavern. She got to her feet, standing on the water, still pierced through by water knives, parallel transparent rods of liquid sharpness that projected from both front and back of her body.

She no longer bled—she had no blood left to bleed.

***

The left side of Batchicken's head was that of a bat, the right side that of a barnyard rooster. It had four eyes, the upper pair a chicken's, the lower a bat's. Its right mouth a beak, its left a twitching whiskered snout.

Its noses, ears, and legs were each divided between its component creatures. It had four wings, the upper set feathered, the lower leathery.

Jenny blinked, confused. She stopped trying to decipher the enigma that was Batchicken.

"I see the Reaper got you again," Batchicken said unsympathetically. "I've told you more than once—escaping from Venice is impossible."

Jenny was confused. "I've been here before?"

"Five hundred and twenty-six times. Why don't you simply *remain* DEAD—be an inquisitor? Hell knows you've the natural aptitude for it." It guffawed. "We're always short-staffed here in Venice—you can have your choice of canal."

***

Jenny glared at Batchicken's miscegenation of parts. *She remembered.*

The Copyrighter-of-the-Year dinner party—the guest of honor had been a cockroach. A big glossy insect wearing a pleated tie and missing its uppermost left leg. It had been seated next to Jenny, on her left. In between bites of chocolate cake and swigs of childbloodwine, they'd made drunken conversation.

"Its economics, madam . . ."

"Most definitely," Jenny giggled drunkenly, unsure what it was talking about.

The door, a red rose, parted like it was blooming on a spring morning and Hatter Sane© walked in with Pink Rabbit© on his arm. Hatter Sane© was actually insane, but he was unable to call himself 'Insane' or 'Mad' Hatter for obvious copyright reasons. This irked him no end.

Pink Rabbit© had had the same copyright problem and so had dyed himself pink to try and avoid litigation. He'd then been told by everyone that he looked female, and so had decided to play-act a female until the dye bleached out again.

Jenny thought he looked disarmingly cute mincing along beside Hatter Sane©.

The pair walked up to and behind Jenny. She made her point of pointedly ignoring them.

"It's economics of course," the cockroach guest of honor opined drunkenly beside her.

"Yesss—" Jenny felt the sudden stab of pain through the left side of her chest, and realized she been shot. She looked back, saw Hatter Sane© smiling down at her. While she gaped in incomprehension, he lifted his razor-gun and kissed its smoking barrel. Then he bent and whispered in Jenny's ear.

"Malice© sends her regards. She says this is payback."

Her heart sliced clean in two, Jenny Loveless took the only way out: she died.

***

"I remember *everything* now. I'm going to find and kill that bitch!" Jenny paced restively around Batchicken, which every now and then was forced to flap its indeterminately positioned wings to get its double-body out of her way.

"You said that the last five hundred and twenty-six times. Can't you simply accept the fact that you're *DEAD*?"

"*NO.*"

"Okay the LIVE door's over there. Weapons too . . ."

***

It went VERY badly: Malice© and the Crimson Queen© were expecting her. A gang of copyrighters ambushed her the moment she stepped through the door. She returned their fire, took pleasure in seeing their bodies explode into blood geysers, fled.

Jenny ran till she reached the quay, stopping there only because it seemed familiar. She thought fast; she needed a hideout, somewhere to scheme how to attack the copyrighters. Then she saw the Grimmer Reaper©.

"*You again?*" the walking shroud sighed at her, its voice the screams of a million ghosts. "Won't you *ever* learn to stay DEAD?"

"Malice© has done me wrong, I want to repay her."

"You blew up Fake-Wonderland©—now we copyrighters have nowhere to live. Were you expecting us to thank you?"

"It was an *accident.*"

"*So?*"

It was speaking so calmly, Jenny almost missed the motion of its foot as it kicked the scythe at her.

She caught sight of the whirling blade and its trajectory at the last reaction-possible moment . . .

Duck Back! OOOOPS! Shiiiiiitttt!!!

***

The river's surface waited patiently for Jenny's body to reach it, waited for the right moment to form its water spears and impale her falling form.

In its liquid depths, her rising reflection grinned, anticipating their next collision.

The mustached gondolier also waited, wondering how long it would take Jenny Loveless to accept the simple fact that no one *ever* escaped from Venice.

God's Refrigerator

Satan, after he'd recovered from the shock of being thrown out of Heaven, crawled out of the crater his impact with Earth had formed, got to his feet and looked around.

He was in a horrid ice landscape. It was COLD: the sun dominating the cloudless sky was both too far away and too small. The only vegetation was ice that had built up into tree formations.

Satan had been badly wounded in the conflict to wrest control of Heaven from God. Viscous white blood dripped from a deep gash over his heart, solidifying into withered reptiles once it touched the floor.

Satan examined his wound. It *hurt*, but he'd heal. His blood reptiles bemused him; usually angel blood bloomed flowers.

There was an ATV parked a short distance away. Wrapping his wings around himself for warmth, he walked over to it. He smiled on seeing the key had been left in the ignition. He climbed into the car and drove off across the ice-scape, looking for something or someone.

A short distance later, he came upon Orbit the Watcher standing beside a building-sized white plastic cube. Orbit was wrapped in something that looked like the hide of a wooly mammoth.

Satan parked his car, got out, and walked over to Orbit.

"What's this?" he asked, shivering, pointing at the huge cube.

"God's fridge," Orbit replied. He noted Satan's bleeding chest. "Sorry, dude, looks like the rebellion didn't go according to plan."

Satan shrugged. "You win some, you lose some." He peered at the monster fridge. "What's in there?"

Orbit grinned. "The Ice Age."

"Huh?"

"Earth's Ice Age, That's why it's so cold everywhere. Orbit pointed a remote control at the huge refrigerator and it swung open. Snowflakes swirled miniature tornados about a huge sphere which rotated in space. It was frozen snowball white, but Satan could still make out continent shapes on it.

Freezing Earth inside, freezing Earth outside.

Satan stood back, avoiding the cold air pouring from the fridge.

Orbit pointed at Satan's dripping wound. "That's a bad cut."

Satan shrugged. "I'll survive—these damned reptile corpses forming from my blood are more trouble than the wound."

He stomped the latest one. With a gunshot crack it disintegrated into chalk.

Then he noticed something else inside the fridge. On a side rack lay a two-pack of bratwurst sausages.

Satan was very amused. "You know, Orb," he said, "God's going to take a very dim view of you keeping your lunch in there along with his latest science project. Better you leave it out here, damnation knows it's freezing enough."

"Lunch? What are you talking about?"

Satan pointed.

Orbit laughed. "That's Man—freeze-dried instant-mix Adam and Eve jelly molds, just add sand, and in Eve's case, a rib."

Satan was interested. "Man?"

"God's new project for when the Ice Age is over." Orbit reached into the rear of the fridge and pulled out a cardboard box. He opened it so Satan could see the contents. "Animals, plants, Tree of Knowledge of Good and Evil seeds . . ."

He shut and replaced the box. "Old guy's got the whole thing figured out. I'm just waiting for the timer . . ."

Satan hardly heard him, his attention was riveted on the pair of Adam and Eve jelly molds. "Man, eh?"

"Yeah, like us angels, only no wings and not as smart."

Satan smiled. It looked like business would be picking up soon. God could keep Heaven, he'd even the score with him here on Earth.

Man would pay hell for what he'd lost.

Outwardly he feigned indifference. "Man, huh? I wonder what the old guy will think up next—ending the world with a flood?"

For a moment Orbit looked uneasy, unsure what to make of that comment, then the two angels burst into simultaneous laughter.

Yeah, Satan was a real character, Orbit thought, too bad his putsch hadn't succeeded.

See you around, Orb," Satan said when the laugher had faded into the ice dunes.

"Yeah, see you round too, dude. Stay out of trouble, willya?"

As if I ever could, Satan thought sourly.

They shook hands, then Satan turned and headed back to his ATV.

And Satan, already making plans to hijack the future, laughed as he walked away from God's refrigerator, bleeding the dinosaur fossils which Man, the new child of God, would one day date with carbon 14.

2012: The Alien Egg

Matt woke up one morning in late August to discover his pillow had become an egg overnight while he slept.

It was a large egg, basketball-sized and soft as a marshmallow, soft as his ex-girlfriend's ass. It was even a light pink in color, just like a marshmallow.

Matt wondered what to do with the egg. Finally, he decided to cook it. It looked large enough to make ten omelets from, so he figured he'd carry the excess omelet to the homeless people's shelter on Sixth Avenue.

Matt carried the soft egg into the kitchen and attempted cracking its shell.

However, because it was so soft, the shell wouldn't crack. So Matt got out a pair of scissors and cut the eggshell open instead.

This worked much better, only Matt now saw that the egg contained a universe inside it—one complete with stars and planets. There were also lots of posters advertising Colonel Sanders Kentucky Fried Chicken inside the egg. And also . . .

Zap!

The laser beam hit Matt right between the eyes. He fell back onto the floor, feeling his brain shredding into mince in the middle of his head as he landed, his face melting so he looked like Freddie Krueger from Nightmare on Elm Street.

"What . . . ?" Matt gasped in pained horror/horrified pain. His horror doubled when a yolk spaceship flew out of the egg. It landed on his kitchen tabletop and opened its top. Two ants in shiny space suits stepped out. Both carried laser pistols larger than themselves. They'd been the ones who'd shot Matt.

The alien ants laughed at Matt.

"Ha ha ha ha ha!" one said. "You're dying."

"Take us to your leader before you expire," the second ant commanded. "We are great fans of President Obama and have important mudslinging news about his opponents which will aid his re-election campaign."

Reelect Obama? Never! Matt thought. With his dying breath, he reached for a can of pesticide and sprayed both ants with it.

"Fuck you bugs, I'm a Republican," he said.

Matt and the ants died together. And the 2012 American presidential elections proceeded as planned, with no one the wiser as to how close the aliens in the egg had come to influencing its outcome.

Retro Race Relations Rumble

Marv, Jake, and Luke put on their costumes. White robes with red cross-patches on them and peaked white hoods. The hoods covered their entire heads, with just a pair of eyeholes cut in them.

"Fuck, man, this is creepy," Luke said. "We look just like the KKK."

"*That* is the whole idea. Stop being such a pussy."

Luke glared at Marv. Marv ignored him, began loading himself with weapons.

Jake got out his slang dictionary, opened it to Racial Insults, thumbed to the 'Negroes' section.

"Nigger," he said softly. The word sounded dirty ugly—like an alligator lurking in a Mississippi swamp. He said it again, inserting a southern drawl: "Neegra . . . dumb neegra . . ."

"Will you *please* stop saying that?" You're freaking me out, Jake."

"You're such a sissy, Luke. This has got to be realistic, okay? Just make sure you don't lose your damn nerve when we pick the neegra up . . ."

"*Stop saying it!*"

"Dude," Marv said softly. "You make one giveaway crack when we pick him up, and I'll shoot you *before* I shoot him."

***

They stopped the hovercar. Overhead the desert sun burned HOT. In the distance a lone tree watched the sands like the ghost of bad things impendent.

Jake, Marv, and Luke pushed the black-hooded man out into the heat. They pushed him along toward the tree, then unhooded him.

Hanson Wayans, middle-aged black businessman, stared at the three Ku Klux Klan members in horror. "I'm telling you I haven't done anything."

"But you did, neegra," Jake said, laughing. "Mah sista Peggy said she done see you ogling her."

Hanson Wayans eyes grew large. "You gentlemen are mistaken; I never . . ." His eyes hardened. "For heaven's sake—this isn't Mississippi in the sixties, what sort of shit is this?"

"Consider this time-travel, *boy*," Jake said, brandishing his knife. "We here don't take kindly to neegras looking at white women."

Hanson gaped at the three Klan members in disbelief. "This is America, this is 2032 . . . You know—I had a dream? What is going on!?"

"Ain't gonna warn ya to curb that sassy tongue again, boy," Marv growled.

Hanson Wayans' bravado drained out of him like diesel from a punctured tank. He stared at his hands. *"Why?"*

"He just don told you dat, nigger," Marv said. "We're your Interracial Time Machine. Now pull down your pants, boy, he got some cuttin' to do."

Luke was sweating bullets. He said nothing; he was ready to cut and run. He'd almost not turned up to execute the plan, but that would have shown him to be yellow.

Jake advanced on the black man, waving his knife menacingly. "I'm gonna cut your balls off, coon, stick em in a cup, watch you bleed like a stuck pig . . . serve you right for eyeing our women."

"Yeah, boy," Marv added, "Can't have you black animals thinkin' ah defiling white purity—thinkin' ah makin' high-yella baboon kids."

"Then we'll string ya up to that tree over there."

"Yeah, *boy*, we gonna have ourselves a sweet southern lynching up north here . . ."

"No you won't," Hanson Wayans said quietly. He'd stopped shaking.

"What you say, boy?" Jake asked, his heart beating faster. "You tryin to sass us again? What you say, *Neegra*!?"

"I SAID: NO, YOU WON'T HAVE A LYNCHING!!!"

It happened almost too fast for the eye to follow. In a rippling split-second of madness, Hanson Wayans expanded into a monster.

A Haman. A seven-foot-tall three-eyed, three-armed, legless thing covered with porcupine quills.

Yawning a mouth full of teeth, tongue slobbering, it leapt at Jake.

Marv was however faster. He stepped between them, letting off a volley of explosive shells at the Haman.

The alien tottered unsteadily for ages, spouting green gore, then it crumbled into the desert sand and dissolved into slime.

Luke discovered he'd peed himself.

***

The atmosphere on the drive back was celebratory.

"The one thing Haman's can't cope with is racial abuse," Jake explained for the umpteenth time. "Apparently on their home world, they were a maltreated minority, got racial abuse aplenty—it's why they fled to Earth."

"It seems a stupid way to become accepted—eating people and taking their place," Marv said.

"So they're stupid. Fuck em, fuck their home world."

"I feel sorry for Mrs. Wayans. I know her—she's a nice lady."

"When he doesn't show, she'll assume he's run off with another woman," Jake said. "Much better than being eaten in her bed one night by the Haman."

Luke said nothing. He was drowning in embarrassment, though his friends had tactfully said nothing about his wet pants.

He knew Jake had the right idea. The government couldn't very well hand guns to everyone and tell them to start insulting (and shooting) everyone they met; could they?

***

They got back into town.

"Hey, Luke," Jake said. "Tomorrow you rent Nazi uniforms—say they're for a play we're doing."

"Shit, Jake. That's what I said the last time. Why'd I always get the bullshit jobs? They're going to be looking at me like—"

"Stop bitching," Marv said. "You knew the score when you joined Interracial Time Machine—Jake does the planning, I handle the weapons, and you're the gofer. How's our organization going to function smoothly if you don't hold up your end—can't even handle a simple rental? And who says you have to get the costumes from the same shop anyway?"

Jake nodded. "We need *authentic* WWII gear, swastikas, lugers, the full works. We'll be skinheads too—we gotta overload on the sort of shit that freaks Jews out: the next Haman's masquerading as a Rabbi down at the old synagogue. I'm just not sure which one he is."

He pulled out his slang dictionary and began to memorize anti-Semitic insults.

The Lionesses and The Hyena

One morning Chris came upon a group of four lionesses arguing over how to share the zebra they had just taken in the hunt.

"I demand the four legs," said the first lioness.

"I demand the four legs," said the second lioness.

"Neither of you shall have them," said the third lioness. "I demand the four legs."

"Oh no," said the fourth lioness. "The four legs are mine."

They argued in this fashion while Chris watched silently, till the noonday sun ruled the sky over the savannah plains, and its heat began to make the flesh of the zebra rot. Still they argued on, with no resolution in sight, till in the end the stink of the rotting zebra caught their attention.

"What a horrible smell," one of them said. "And to think we were actually considering eating this animal, my sisters. Thank heavens we hadn't yet reached any agreement. Come . . . let us go for another hunt; all the zebra are gone now, but maybe we'll be able to catch a little antelope or at worst a hare to still the pangs of hunger till tomorrow."

The remaining three lionesses agreed with her and they left.

Watching their departure was a hungry hyena. When they were well out of sight it came out of hiding and sniffed the carcass of the zebra.

"What a lovely smell," it said.

The hyena went away and called three others.

"Come quickly, sisters," it said. "A delicious zebra meal is waiting for us, and best of all, it still has all four legs, so we can each of us have one to eat."

Shaking his head, Chris walked away.

The Secret Life of Drawers

Black, White, Red, and Thong were four sisters forced by circumstances into living together. Though they didn't get along, they had no choice but to pretend to.

All four were panties, property of Miss Lucy D—.

***

Being a panty is an occasionally romantic, but generally so-so existence. Though a little on the large side, Lucy's buttocks were shapely and the panties didn't mind the little bit of stretching involved in being worn by her, considering it exercise. But after a while the excitement wears off in even the most interesting jobs.

Today Red was in an atrocious mood, this happened on average once a month—she'd get up and hold court like she was doing now, declaiming on the pros and cons of being underwear of a particular color or function.

Shocking-pink Thong, considered a slut by the other three, usually got the worst of Red's ire. This was ironic, as of the four she cared the least what was said about her. So what if she was a whore? She had a pleasant life.

"Don't you have *any* self-esteem?" Red was saying now. "At least try to cover Lucy better—all guys do is pull you to one side and they're in. "'Easy Access Baby' I hear they call you. And you're even easier from *behind*. Now I'd like to see some son-of-a-bitch try that sort of shit with *me!*"

These weren't simply idle words. Red was sturdily built, looking almost like a pair of shorts. She was also doubly reinforced at the crotch—no way was any dumb prick going to get into Lucy when Red was on duty.

Thong said nothing. Though she hated Red, she considered it beneath her dignity to take her up on the issue of who was better at assguard duty.

Besides, she wasn't complaining—she got used more than the others (which she *knew* Red was jealous of), had lots of expensive wining and dining, travel, lots of hot sex with lots of hunky boxers, and hung out with the Jet Set. She also got complimented a lot on how well she looked on Lucy, or rather how good Lucy looked in her.

She however felt sorry for Black. Thong knew she'd be permanently suicidal if she had Black's life.

"Hey, Red, take it easy on Thong, it's not her fault she's the way she is," Black said. She always stood up for the others, a lifetime of ill-use had made her humble and nice.

Red, angry at being denied her favorite target, rounded on her angrily. "And who's going to make me? *You*—the pong patrol? Bitch, I was *coming* to you, but I see you're as impatient for abuse as ever. Girl, if I was you I'd *kill* myself; what kind of a sorry-ass excuse for a life do you have?"

Black was Lucy's shit-panty. She only ever got used when the boss had diarrhea or some fart-inducing syndrome, or was ill—in short anything which might make her soil herself, except one. Once, when the mistress had a running stomach, White had sat next to Black in the wash-bin and had fainted from the smell coming from her. And then there'd been that time also when Lucy had had that fungal infection. Black had stunk of antibiotics for days even after several washes.

And Red *loved* to rub it in her face.

"You're the lowest of the low, Black. Don't you ever dare stick your stinking—yes *literally* stinking—mouth in my business again."

Black burst into tears and crawled off weeping to her corner of the drawer. White followed after her to comfort her, though keeping on her less smelly side.

***

White returned from comforting Black.

"Red, that was *nasty*. Why'd you have to give the girl such a hard time? Thong's right, it's not her fault she's what she is. We should support her, not knock her down. None of us three would exchange jobs with her, and if anything happens to her we might be forced—"

"Hold it right there, you fake prude. I've had it up to here with your white-is-right bullshit. Who're you to lecture me? Fuck you, you think you're so good, eh?"

"I was only trying to . . ."

And don't you keep pretending you're *pure*, better than the rest of us just because Lucy only wears you to church and weddings and funerals."

"*I am* pure!" White insisted indignantly."

"Tell that to the manufacturer, bitch. I *smelt* you the last time we were in the wash-bin together—that time she came back from the wedding? *All* women get horny at weddings. Those stains on you weren't milk, were they? They were cum—*semen*. Stop putting on airs—You're as much a slut as Thong here. Religious hypocrite!"

With that parting shot, she turned stiffly (Lucy had washed her with the wrong detergent last month and she *was* stiff) and made her way over to *her* corner, the one opposite Black's.

White stared after her in unconcealed disgust. Red's tirade had hurt her, being true—Lucy did tend to get laid a lot at weddings.

"I really feel for Black, her life has to be hell," she whispered to Thong, who'd begun doing some push-ups to keep in shape for the hunky boxers. "And Red never stops fucking with her. What's wrong with Red anyway?"

Thong paused her motions. "I'm not *sure* . . . Hey, hold on a sec . . ."

She peered out of the drawer for a few minutes, studying the wall calendar, noting the marked dates. Finally she nodded and withdrew back inside. She laughed.

"It's alright, darling," she called sweetly to Red, now indignantly ensconced in her corner of their drawer. "It's no sin to be premenstrual. Lucy'll be here to give you your monthly airing shortly."

The Devil in Utopia

I

You sail through the night skies of Decapolis like the Grim Reaper herself, a winged smear of evil intentions.

Today's mission is simple:

"My sister Habiba Farouk is having an affair," Latifa Shabazz says, "You will find out whom with."

She smiles the cold evil smile you find so erotic, and you know that once his identity is known, her sister's lover's name will immediately head an 'urgent attention' list of those accused of 'Error,' probably even of those plotting to murder the glorious Tyrant and sovereign, Xerxes III himself.

Latifa Shabazz *hates* her beautiful older sister. Unable to stand seeing her happy, she makes it her business to ensure misfortune follows Habiba around.

Misfortune such as the 'accidental' deaths of her two previous husbands.

Once her new lover is arrested, Habiba will naturally run to Latifa seeking assistance in securing his release—assistance Latifa won't render.

***

You fly, as indistinguishable from the night to eye or radar as a drop of black ink.

Your destination is the suburb of Yaafour, where lie the weekend villas of rich merchants and princes, men normally too rich to be accused of Error.

Not in this case, however. The look in the Minister of Torture's eyes when she gave you this assignment was adamant. You love that horrid look, the insane eyes illuminating her unbeautiful leeched violence-jaded face—your infernal lust for Latifa Shabazz is the primary reason you continue to work for the Utopian government. She is more inhumane than any female of your own type—you are Djinn—you've ever encountered.

Your payment for your work for the Ministry of Torture—the corpses of the guilty dead—isn't bad either.

It is primarily your desire for the icy Latifa Shabazz, however, that keeps you here.

II

You occupy the period spent flying to Yaafour with reflection.

Since the coup d'état that ousted the decadent democratics in 2010 (twelve years ago), with its re-establishment of the monarchy, things in Utopia have been *much* better.

Accompanying the reintroduction of aristocracy has been the royal crusade for 'ethical purity'—'ethical correctness' as opposed to its political sibling so espoused by American decadentry. Ensuring the success of this crusade has necessitated the establishment of the Ministry of Torture, with its associated reopening of the ancient Decapolitan dungeons to the public and reacquainting them with their functions.

The chorused screams of pain filtering daily through the sealed doors lining the corridors of the Ethics Ministry perfectly fill the space your missing soul would have occupied.

***

It hasn't been all smooth sailing for Utopia however.

Amnesty International has them on sixteen human rights violations lists. They naturally decry the actions of the Ministry of Torture—despite Latifa Shabazz's endless press conferences explaining their suspicions of brutality away.

"The name is Orwellian in origin," she always says. "In George Orwell's seminal work '1984', Oceania gives its ministries names opposite to their true function: the Ministry of Peace for example, is responsible for waging war; the Ministry of Love for maintaining law and order.

"We've just done similarly—our Ministry of Torture is primarily concerned with 'pain relief' . . . good works . . . call it charity if you prefer."

Lies of course.

And the UN?

Xerxes III is a wise sovereign, adept at softly speaking the right words in the right ears at the right time.

He already has Utopia's next door neighbors, the Israelis, eating out of his hands with his suggestion that Utopia may be willing to cede them uncontested possession of the Gibran oil fields, and even help resolve their 'Palestinian Problem,' in return for Israeli assistance with the fledgling Utopian nuclear energy project.

The Americans are of course incensed by this, with several right-wing religious groups going so far as to label Xerxes III the Antichrist.

III

You alight from the night amidst landscaped lawns and oases of date palms.

Habiba Farouk's lover is unwise. His palatial villa has only three guards. There may be no need even to add him to the list of Errorists. You could kill him yourself . . .

That, however, isn't today's job. It may be tomorrow's.

You locate the master bedroom. You shift shape to liquid, and like rain leaking through a hole in cracked concrete, drip into place, overlaying yourself finally as a transparent layer over the paint above the headboard of their huge bed.

The bedroom door opens and Habiba enters with her lover. You're shocked for a long time when you see who it is—the glorious Tyrant, Xerxes III himself.

You shrug; men will be men, women, women. Your mission is over before it's begun.

You wait and listen, however. Post-coital talk is usually very revealing—once past her fits of rage over her hated sister's honeypot snaring the ultimate bee, Latifa Shabazz will appreciate information concerning any planned nuptials.

You may even earn yourself a bonus allocation of corpse flesh.

For a while nothing more happens. Xerxes and Habiba behave like men and women do in such situations, while you watch like you're assigned to.

When their carnal pleasure is over, however, the real fun starts. The bedroom door bursts off its hinges, and Xerxes's three bodyguards burst in, guns blazing.

It is an assassination attempt.

"What is the meaning of this . . . ?" is all Xerxes manages to say before bullets silence him.

Your primary thought now is to save Habiba. You solidify off the walls into demon shape and wade through the attacker's fusillade of bullets, and then through *them*, slicing all three to shreds of red meat in under a minute.

You return your attention to the couple.

His Majesty Xerxes III is undeniably dead—the top half of his head no longer exists.

He has dripping brains for hair.

Habiba Farouk is unharmed, though staring at you as if she's seeing a demon. You remember that she is, and quickly shift shape back down to human form.

(Your preferred shape for social interaction is that of a pot-bellied middle-aged man in a short-sleeved brown gabardine suit with a red fez and an ingratiating smile. A minor government official. You've discovered such a look instils a disarming sense of superiority in those you meet.)

"Do not be alarmed, madam," you say in an intentionally timid voice, "the danger is now over."

In response, Habiba just stutters, "Who . . . who . . . who . . . ?"

You realize changing shape in front of her has made matters worse. Habiba Farouk now looks like she would like to lose her mind but cannot figure out how to.

You are concerned for Habiba and her state of mental health. In this hour of national tragedy, she is the only witness—her testimony is crucial.

The *only* witness—suddenly you understand what you must do to protect this great society.

With a kind smile, you bend over Habiba and rip her beautiful head off her shoulders.

You're amused by the look of reproach frozen in her dead eyes.

"Who . . . who . . . who . . . ?" she fish-mouths at you before she's all out of air and her eyes go dull.

You drop her head beside her body.

Next, you study Xerxes III's body.

With minor effort you reshape yourself in his image. The only tricky part of this process is matching your voice box to his, but by gripping his throat and meticulously tracing its contours, you finally succeed in this too. You smile when you say your first words in his voice:

"I am Xerxes III."

IV

You survey the room.

What to do with the real Xerxes's corpse? After a moment's reflection you shred it into unrecognizable chunks and mingle it with the fragments of his guards/assassins.

You quickly see how this creates a problem—there will be too many bones if anyone is pedantic/stupid enough to attempt reassembling the corpses.

Three people cannot have forty fingers or toes between them. Or four hearts.

(You realize you should have eaten Xerxes instead, but you weren't hungry, and it's too late now—impossible to tell which part of him is which any more.)

Mentally, you upgrade the number of attackers to four—one a naked pervert intent on raping your concubine, Habiba. He was apelike, strong enough to rip off her head.

You smile.

You *are* now Xerxes III, King of Utopia.

Admittedly, you lack his memories, but this is easily fixed. You think open a deep bullet-gash in your forehead; this will account for your temporary/prolonged amnesia.

(This also solves the problem of remembering how you survived the attack yourself, and *how* your attackers became chunks of meat. A few dazed-eyed mutters of 'djinn, djinn' will suffice to convey the illusion of divine intervention, as well as mark you as God's chosen.)

Satisfied, you dress in the erstwhile monarch's clothes.

V

Will you be a better Tyrant than the dead Xerxes III? You think so.

You've long had plans for the improvement of Utopia.

You've always disagreed with the idea that it is sufficient that people are *seen* to behave right, that healthy actions are symptoms of ethically correct mentalities.

Error is like cancer, you believe, even a little is way too much.

Similarly, Error is like pregnancy—no one is ever 'just a little bit' so.

Measures must be taken to *ensure* the people of Utopia think *correct thoughts*.

You will introduce days of scheduled monthly torture for each of your glorious citizens, a day when, with the help of purifying pain, the secrets of individual hearts will be laid bare.

Like the Catholic ritual of confession, but much more reliable.

Yes!

Certainly, your new policies will create outcry and statements of 'not acceptable' at the United Nations, but that can't be helped. Tempting deals on underpriced oil and gas to the permanent Security Council members will calm most ruffled humane feathers.

What is *most* important is to keep the Americans mollified.

You are Djinn after all; temptation/wish-fulfilment is your species' stock in trade.

Already you see your glorious reign stretch for thousands of millennia.

But you're getting well ahead of yourself.

First things first. Every monarch needs a queen, and while Xerxes's queen Fatima is indeed gorgeous, the ghoulish Latifa Shabazz is much more to your taste.

Considering her inhumaneness, you are certain Latifa Shabazz will enjoy being queen. You will even permit her to continue to head the Ministry of Torture after your wedding.

(Latifa will certainly be displeased by the news of her sister's death. Being queen, she'd have had much greater scope to cause her misery. It can't be helped, however.)

With a pleased smile, you pick up the phone and call the palace to announce the unsuccessful assassination attempt on your life.

ABOUT THE AUTHOR

Wol-vriey is Nigerian, and quite tall.

He currently resides in a state of uneasy stalemate with his threatening-to-thin-beyond-redemption hair, and believes there actually are things that go bump in the night.

Wol-vriey recycles the ridiculous into reasonable reality for the reader.

His WEIRRRD philosophy?

WEIRRRD = Warp/Write Everything into Realistic Ridiculous Readable Distorted Dream Dimension Descriptions.

Wol-vriey blogs at:

http://oddityfarm.wordpress.com

OTHER GREAT TITLES FROM

Burning Bulb
PUBLISHING

WWW.BURNINGBULBPUBLISHING.COM

WOL-VRIEY
BIZARRO AND TRANSGRESSIVE FICTION

BOSTON POSH

In 2028 AD, the USA is a nation ravaged by hungry dragons and dinosaurs. In Boston, Massachusetts, private eye Bud Malone is hired to rescue a kidnapped heiress. But nothing is as it seems.

Malone works to unravel a tangled web involving Boston Chinatown, a 200-year-old woman with a 9-year-old body, white robots, a human-liver-eating psychopath, a golem, a porcelain dragon, and a snake goddess with a crush on him. There's also a woman obsessed with chicken sex. Then Malone meets Posh Lane, a gorgeous call girl who's desperate to quit her pimp.

Romantic sparks ignite between Posh and Malone, but Posh's past suddenly catches up with her in a BIG way. To save Posh, Malone agrees to run a quest for Earth's new rulers, the Forks. But, Malone has no idea that agreeing to the Fork's odd request will send him on the weirdest trip he's ever been on in his life.

VAGINA MUNDI

Rachel Risk is a professional thief with super-strong hair that can stretch like tentacles to manipulate objects. Ashley Status has both a digitally augmented brain, and 'muscle-purses' in her arms and legs in which she stores inflatable objects—cars, guns, rocket launchers, etc.

When Raye is framed as the fall girl in a jewel robbery, the pair flee Chicago's vengeful robot gangsters and take refuge in the Hotel Bizarre, where the gorgeous 'vagina singer,' Femina, is performing for a week.

But the Hotel Bizarre is even stranger than its name suggests, and very soon Raye and Ash are involved in an deadly adventure, a struggle for survival the likes of which they'd never imagined possible—with loads of deviant sex, drugs, music, and violence at every turn. And just what is the old woman in the skin desert really doing with all those cats glued to her walls?

Vagina Mundi—a Bizarro Hymn in praise of WOMAN!

Burning Bulb
PUBLISHING

WOL-VRIEY
BIZARRO AND TRANSGRESSIVE FICTION

VEGAN VAMPIRE VAGINAS

The biggest bank heist in US history. And Tom Palmer can't remember pulling it off. And no, this isn't your standard case of amnesia. After a one-night-stand gone horribly wrong, Boston salesman Tom Palmer wakes up with a vagina implanted in his left hand. Then his day gets worse.

Tom is transported across space-time to a nightmare version of Boston, one where the Bizarro virus has transformed half the population into cannibals. Worst of all, Tom discovers that in this new Boston, he's the infamous gangster Pussypalm, wanted for robbing the Federal Reserve Bank of Boston a year ago. He also learns that the vagina in his hand is prophetic, i.e. it talks . . . after sex.

With 130 people left dead during his bank heist and six billion dollars missing, Tom knows he's living on borrowed time. It is in his best interests not to remember anything. Because once he does . . .

VEGAN ZOMBIE APOCALYPSE

In the post-apocalypse worlderness, zombies rule the earth. They're allergic to meat, and brains literally make them explode. Zombies now eat blood potatoes, parasitic tubers grown in the flesh of humancows corralled in maximum security farms. Two fugitives meet in the ancient ruins of Texas. The first is Soil 15-f, a womancow who's escaped her farm a week before she's due to be killed and her blood potato crop harvested. The second fugitive is Able Kane, former head necros food technician, now sentenced to death for heresy. But Soil is no ordinary humancow.

Unknown to herself, she's the vegan zombie agricultural revolution, and the zombies desperately want her back. And the necros equally desperately want Able Kane dead. He's fled with a forbidden discovery which will reshape the world for the worse if used. And Able is just hardheaded/misguided enough to use it.

Burning Bulb
PUBLISHING

ANTHOLOGIES
BIZARRO AND TRANSGRESSIVE FICTION

THE BIG BOOK OF BIZARRO

The Big Book of Bizarro brings together the peculiar prose of an international cast of the most grotesquely-gonzo, genre-grinding modern writers who ever put pen to paper (or mouse to pad), including:

NIGHT OF THE LIVING DEAD horror writers John Russo & George Kosana; HUSTLER MAGAZINE erotica contributors Eva Hore, Andrée Lachapelle, & J. Troy Seate and established Bizarro genre authors D. Harlan Wilson, William Pauley III, Wol-vriey, Laird Long, Richard Godwin and so many more!

From Alien abductions to Zombie sex, The Big Book of Bizarro contains OVER FIFTY STORIES of the most outrélandish transgressive fiction that you'll ever lay your capricious and curious hands upon!

WARNING: This book may be one of the most controversial and dangerous books you'll ever read.

WESTWARD HOES

Nine outlaw writers rode into town from obscurity to pen nine tantalizing tales of horror and fantasy, and leaving once they branded their own personal marks on the weird western genre and became living legends of the American Frontier experience.

Like drunken Indian scouts, the writers fervidly tracked down and captured the Western genre, tore off its fashionable veneer and ravished its exposed essence.

So belly up to the bar with your favorite soiled dove and enjoy perusing these thrilling tales of Old West debauchery, danger and desire; compiled by the publisher of The Big Book of Bizarro and featuring the bizarro novella *Big Trouble in Little Ass* by Wol-vriey.

Burning Bulb
PUBLISHING

ANTHOLOGIES
BIZARRO AND TRANSGRESSIVE FICTION

THE BIG BOOK OF BIZARRO SPECIAL KINDLE EDITIONS

OTHER AWESOME COLLECTIONS

GARY LEE VINCENT'S
DARKENED
THE WEST VIRGINIA VAMPIRE SERIES

DARKENED HILLS

When evil descends on a small West Virginia town, who will survive?

Jonathan did not start out his life to become a rambler, it just worked out that way. William was a troubled youth with something to hide. Both were from Melas, a small town tucked away in the West Virginia hills... a town where disappearances are happening more and more frequently.

After the suicide of a wanted serial killer, the townsfolk thought the nightmare was over. But when a centuries-old vampire is discovered they find out the hard way it's just getting started. Dark secrets can only stay hidden for so long and when the devil comes to collect, there will be hell to pay. Can Jonathan and William find a way to stop the vampire before it's too late? Find out in *Darkened Hills!*

DARKENED HOLLOWS

In the heart-stopping sequel to the award-winning *Darkened Hills*, Jonathan and William must return to West Virginia to face possible criminal charges stemming from their last visit to the damned town of Melas, where both had narrowly escaped the clutches of a vampire seethe.

And as livestock start mysteriously getting murdered with all of their blood drained, worried farmers are searching for answers - leaving the local Sheriff and his deputy racing against time to learn the cause before a more violent crime is committed.

Burning Bulb
PUBLISHING

WWW.DARKENEDHILLS.COM

GARY LEE VINCENT'S
DARKENED
THE WEST VIRGINIA VAMPIRE SERIES

DARKENED WATERS

When the world goes to hell, the chosen must arise!

As Talman Cane orchestrates a flood of epic proportions in this third installment of the *Darkened* series the towns of Melas and Tarklin are caught completely off guard by the deluge. Hell-bent on finishing what they started, the evil brothers return to the lunatic asylum to take care of the witnesses and add to the ever-growing army of the undead.

Aided by Lucifer himself and the insane vampire demon Legion, the stage is set to channel all of the forces of hell to come forth. In an all-out race to survive, Jonathan, William, and Amanda soon discover they are up against impossible odds as Lucifer opens the Gateway to Hell, ushering in the zombie apocalypse and the End Times.

DARKENED SOULS

Melas and the Madison House are about to be rebuilt.
True evil is about to be reborne!

Young ex-priest and vampire-killer William is drawn back to the West Virginian town that almost killed him, where his vampire arch-enemy Victor Rothenstein still stalks the earth.

The town of Melas lies destroyed after the battle of the End of Days. But why is wealthy Jackie Nixon so eager to rebuild it using the bone dust of murdered souls?

Terrible evil has visited before, but the Gateway to Hell is about to be reopened in a horrific climax. And this time – it's personal.

www.DARKENEDHILLS.com

Burning Bulb
PUBLISHING

RISE OF THE DEAD

AN EARTH-SHATTERING ANTHOLOGY OF ZOMBIE TERROR

Featuring Stories By:

John A. Russo   Tyson Blue   E.L. Stice   Nelson W. Pyles

Andy Rausch   Stephen Spignesi   R.D. Riley   Zakary McGaha

David J. Fairhead   Gary Lee Vincent   David C. Hayes   Rachel Montgomery

Paul Victor Wargelin   David F. Walker   William Vitka

Rich Bottles Jr.   Douglas Brode

RISE OF THE DEAD - a collection of seventeen
tales of unspeakable zombie terror. Featuring a foreword and
short story by John A. Russo!

www.TheJohnRusso.com

Burning Bulb
PUBLISHING

THE BOOBY HATCH

With NIGHT OF THE LIVING DEAD, John Russo helped blaze a path in the horror genre that has never been equalled. In this hillarious erotic novel, he blazes a path through the wild, zany Sex Revolution of the 1970s.

Sweet, innocent Cherry Jankowski works for Joyful Novelties, where she tests sex toys ranging from the ridiculous to the sublime. But she can't find love or peace of mind and her efforts are hampered by a Peeping Tom, an exhibitionist, a cross-dressing boyfriend, a quack psychiatrist, and even her own product-testing partner, Marcello Fettucini, who can't get it up anymore and is scared of losing his job!

www.TheJohnRusso.com

Burning Bulb
PUBLISHING

WEST VIRGINIA-THEMED HUMORROROTICA

BY RICH BOTTLES JR.

HELLHOLE WEST VIRGINIA

From the heights of Mothman's perch high atop the Silver Bridge in Point Pleasant to the depths of Hellhole Cavern in Pendleton County, evil lurks within the shadows as the sun sets upon the haunted hills and hollows of West Virginia.

Bizarro author Rich Bottles Jr. blows the coffin lid off horror genre clichés with this tour de force cast of Eco-friendly vampires, beach-yearning zombies and sex-starved she-devils.

LUMBERJACKED

If you are easily offended or do not possess a truly depraved sense of humor, this story may not be the light summer reading fare you desire. As for the four feisty female freshmen stranded on top of West Virginia's third highest mountain, they have no choice but to experience the sick, twisted debauchery and perverted mayhem described deep inside the tight unbroken bindings of this horrific missive.

Lumberjacked takes the reader to a nightmarish world where character development and aesthetic integrity are prematurely cut short by the swinging axes of maniacal lumberjacks, who are hell bent on death and destruction in the remote forests of Appalachia. And at the climax, when paranoia crosses over to the paranormal, Lumberjacked makes Deliverance look like a family raft trip down the Lower Gauley.

THE MANACLED

What happens when twin brothers lease out the former West Virginia State Penitentiary with the false purpose of filming a documentary on supernatural phenomena, but their true intention is to make a pornographic movie?

Chaos ensues as the disturbed spirits of murdered convicts, along with the reanimated dead from the neighboring Indian Burial Mound, take their vengeance on the unwary and undressed trespassers.

Zombies, ghosts, mobsters and porn collide in this bizarro tale from horror author Rich Bottles Jr.

Burning Bulb
PUBLISHING

THE MOST FRIGHTENING MOVIE
EVER MADE IS NOW A NOVEL!

night OF THE LIVING DEAD

JOHN A. RUSSO

NIGHT OF THE LIVING DEAD

Why does **Night of the Living Dead** hit with such chilling impact?
Is it because everyday people in a commonplace house are suddenly the
victims of a monstrous invasion? Or is it because the ghouls who surround
the house with grasping claws were once ordinary people, too?

Decide for yourself as you read, and the horror grips you. All the
cannibalism, suspense and frenzy of the smash-hit move are here in the
novel.

www.TheJohnRusso.com

Burning Bulb
PUBLISHING

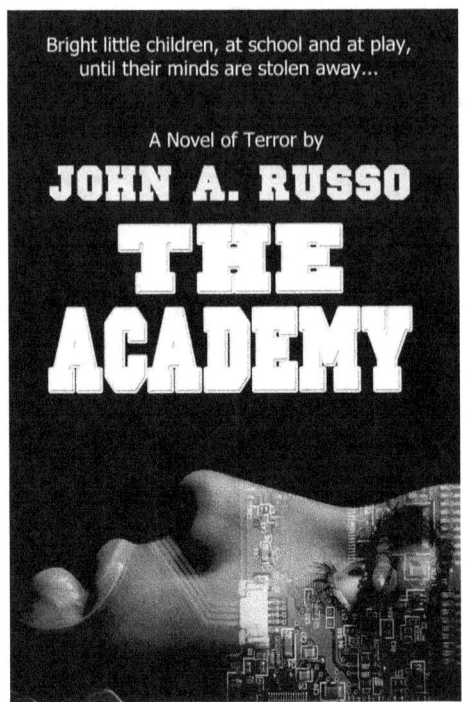

Bright little children, at school and at play, until their minds are stolen away...

A Novel of Terror by

JOHN A. RUSSO

THE ACADEMY

THE ACADEMY

The Academy. It's every parent's dream, turning their little darlings into geniuses, superachievers, perfect little children.

And if there's a problem, the Academy fixes that too. It's a simple operation. Just a little device. Then a teeny pink scar on a tender little skull . . .

One boy knows the secret. Now he wants his mind back. But it's much, much too late. Too late for anything but the ugly feelings. The bad feelings. The messy sexy feelings. The knife-cold hatred, the murderous rage, for total, screaming, blood-drenching revenge . . .

www.TheJohnRusso.com

Burning Bulb
PUBLISHING

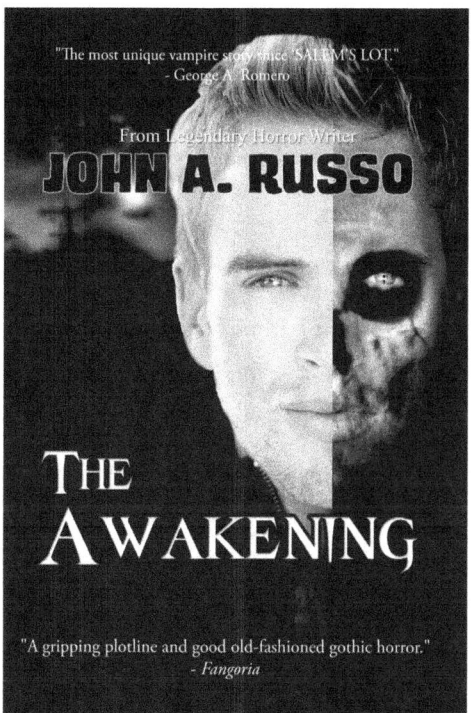

"The most unique vampire story since 'SALEM'S LOT."
- George A. Romero

From Legendary Horror Writer
JOHN A. RUSSO

THE
AWAKENING

"A gripping plotline and good old-fashioned gothic horror."
- Fangoria

THE AWAKENING

For two hundred years, he has rested. Now he rises. Now he will be satisfied. Nothing can stop him. No one can resist him.

Benjamin Latham is young and handsome, his eighteenth-century mind wakened to a bizarre twentieth-century world. And there is the need deep within . . . an animal need, frightening, murderous, unholy . . . a vital need that must be fed.

And with his need comes a power over men and women to do his bidding, to quiet his dark craving . . .

Until the murders begin. And the inquiries. All suggesting the same hideous truth.

Now Benjamin must find a sanctuary: a lover, a partner, a friend. Someone who can share his darkness. Someone he can lead to . . . The Awakening.

www.TheJohnRusso.com

Burning Bulb
PUBLISHING

DEALEY PLAZA

From legendary horror and suspense writer JOHN RUSSO comes a harrowing tale where no one is safe!

Dealey Plaza is one of the most notorious places in America, and when youthful conspiracy buffs go there in 1964 to stage their own reenactment of the Kennedy Assassination, four of them are brutally murdered ~ the first victims of a hate-filled legacy that continues for four more decades.

The survivors of that long-ago Dallas trip, each of them now icons of the American way of life, are about to be honored ~ or killed.

Who will live and who will die? Will it be country-western star Lori McCoy? Her loving husband? Her scheming ex-husband? Or the case-hardened FBI agent and longtime friend who risks his life trying to protect them?

www.DealeyPlazaBook.com

From Legendary Horror Writer
JOHN A. RUSSO

LIMB TO LIMB

SUCH A PRETTY GIRL . . .
Tiffany Blake was a beautiful long-limbed dancer with a glorious future and the backing of a rich benefactor. Then a monstrous accident severed her leg at the hip.

SUCH A COLD, CRUEL KNIFE . . .
And now her fellow dancers are disappearing without a trace. One by one they fall victim to a dark and deadly pattern of evil – caught by the bloody, brutal logic that would have them pay with their lovely bodies for the cruel fate of another . . .victims of the sadistic madman whose flashing knife will make them writhe a gruesome new dance.

www.TheJohnRusso.com

Burning Bulb
PUBLISHING

LIVING THINGS

Beneath the shimmering Miami sun sprawls one of the Mafia's biggest empires, a glittering world of lavish beachfront mansions, neon-painted nightclubs, beautiful women, expensive cars—and absolute control over the state's billion-dollar drug trade. But, one by one, its ganglords and henchmen are falling prey to a new rival. His powers are fueled by monstrous ancient rituals; his hellish undead legions slaughter mobsters and innocent citizens alike, his unholy lust for power is virtually unstoppable.

Now a burned-out ex-detective and a brilliant anthropologist must enter a gruesome, nightmare world to fight this master of malevolence and illusion. Their time is short, their weapons few, and they face an ultimate, terrifying choice - annihilation or the loss of their souls to the eternal torment of those who never die. . .

www.TheJohnRusso.com

Burning Bulb
PUBLISHING

MAD WORLD BY ANDY RAUSCH

"*Mad World* is dark, twisted, no-holds-barred fun."
—Jason Starr, author of *Bust*, *Slide*, and *The Max*

EVERYONE'S PLAYING AN ANGLE IN THE CITY OF ANGELS

Mad World tells the stories of a black hitman who doubles as a
university professor, a Catholic priest who longs to be a gangster,
a would-be author from Kansas, a gay phone sex operator who
claims he's straight, a group of rich twentysomethings playing a
deadly game of life and death, a vicious Mafia boss, and a sleazy
Hollywood movie director. As each of their stories intersect, the
body count piles up and the action comes nonstop in this tense,
white-knuckle thriller by first-time author Andy Rausch.

"A wild ride. If you like it gangster, *Mad World* delivers."
—Daniel Birch, author of *Get Some*

Burning Bulb
PUBLISHING

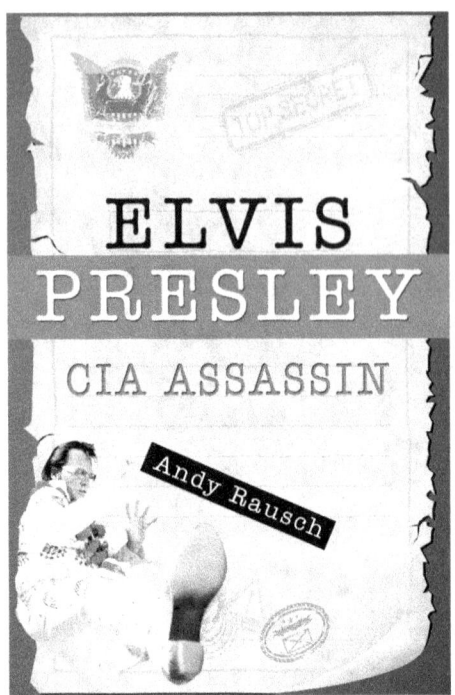

ELVIS PRESLEY, CIA ASSASSIN

"I can guarantee you. Read this book and you'll never look at Elvis the same way again!"
~ Douglas Brode, author of ELVIS CINEMA AND POPULAR CULTURE

SOON TO BE A MAJOR MOTION PICTURE

In 1970, singer Elvis Presley secretly met with President Richard Nixon. This new comedic novel imagines that Presley became a Central Intelligence Agency operative, eventually moving up through the ranks to become a skilled assassin.

Presented in an oral history fashion, the book tells us about Presley's secret transformation by the people who knew him best.

Did he fake his death in 1977? Was Presley involved with the Watergate scandal? The Iran hostage crisis? Communicating with aliens?

Read this book to find out the answers to these and many more questions.

Burning Bulb
PUBLISHING

THE TAILSMAN

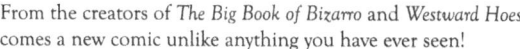

From the creators of *The Big Book of Bizarro* and *Westward Hoes* comes a new comic unlike anything you have ever seen!

He's hot on the trail, looking for some *tail...*

Sly Franko was a man of the West, a forger of the wild frontier. Like the Country Western song that would be written years after he died, the words, "Faster horses, younger women, and more money," seemed to be the anthem of this horn dog cowboy.

Franko would ride into town on a blazing saddle, find the closest saloon to wet the whistle, belly up to a good card game, and find him a hot-loving hussy to get his cowpoke on with.

However, Sly might have met his match when a visit to bathroom leads to terror and death. Can Sly and his poker buddies solve the mystery before more of the townsfolk are murdered? Find out in this exciting premier issue of *The Tailsman*!

WWW.BURNINGBULBCOMICS.COM

THE HAGS OF BLACK COUNTY

by Michelle Bowser

Ruled by a committee of Hags, and fueled by toothless rivalries, Black County lurks just far enough out of the way to be completely unnoticed by the rest of civilization. Its inhabitants have been mentally warped for generations and the land itself seems to have the power to drive anyone unlucky enough to visit into ridiculous hillbilly madness. When a construction Company needs to bury a pipeline through its ludicrous hills and valleys, a twisted charm goes to work and every aspect of already bizarre Black County life takes a gory turn for the hysterical. Take a preposterous trip along with its citizens, both native and new, through escapades such as the Hag parade, the grand opening of Madame Skunk's House of Ill Repute, the demolition derby riot and the rabid, zombie clown apocalypse.

THE ABANDONED SOUL

by Daniel Sellers

After spending most of his 20s in a drug and alcohol fueled daze, a young man finally hits rock bottom. Having used up his friends and their good graces, he ends up squatting in an abandoned house. Forcibly sobering he begins to realize that he is not alone in this abandoned house. Left with one last friend and a mountain of regrets, he must decide if this presence is a guilty conscience, or a malicious hunter.

WE WISH YOU A HAPPY KILLDAY

by Jason Heroux

"We Wish You a Happy Killday" is the story of an international b eloved holiday called "Killday" where one day a year everyone over the age of fifteen is permitted to register for a license allowing them to kill one other person. But this year Chad Ovenstock doesn't feel like killing anyone. His friends and family urge him to participate in the festivities, but he can't seem to get into the holiday spirit. On the day before Killday Chad comes in contact with Ambrose, an old friend who suffered a nervous breakdown and is now part of The One Ant Army, a mysterious cult dedicated to making the future disappear. When the holiday finally arrives Chad refuses to participate and tries to survive on his own, surrounded by constant gunfire, countless corpses, and the nagging suspicion that Ambrose may have secretly brainwashed him into becoming a member of The One Ant Army cult.

Burning Bulb
PUBLISHING

www.ingramcontent.com/pod-product-compliance
Lightning Source LLC
Chambersburg PA
CBHW071303130626
46556CB00003B/1444